John Lang (b. 1816), writer, newspaper editor, traveller and barrister, lived in India for a number of years. A prominent lawyer of his time, he most notably appeared for the Rani of Jhansi against the British East India Company. He was also the editor and publisher of the periodical, *Mofussilite*.

Lang's published work includes *The Wetherbys* (1853), *Too Clever by Half* (1853), *Too Much Alike* (1854), *The Forger's Wife* (1855), *Captain Macdonald* (1856), *Will He Marry Her* (1858), *The Ex-Wife* (1858), *My Friend's Wife* (1859), *The Secret Police* (1859) and *Botany Bay; or True Stories of the Early Days of Australia* (1859).

John Lang died in Mussooric in 1864.

the *himalaya club*

AND OTHER ENTERTAINMENTS
FROM THE RAJ

JOHN LANG

SPEAKING
TIGER

SPEAKING TIGER
An imprint of FEEL Books Pvt. Ltd
4381/4, Ansari Road, Daryaganj,
New Delhi–110002, India

Edition copyright © Speaking Tiger 2015

ISBN: 978-93-85288-34-0
eISBN: 978-93-85288-17-3

10 9 8 7 6 5 4 3 2 1

Typeset in Adobe Jenson Pro by SÜRYA, New Delhi
Printed at Sanat Printers, New Delhi

Contents

Foreword by Ruskin Bond   *vii*

The Himalaya Club   1

Military Matters   26

The Himalayas   55

Returning   81

Miscellaneous   104

Forward   121

FOREWORD

In Search of John Lang

I HAD LIVED in Mussoorie just over four years without realizing that someone of literary distinction might be buried in the old English cemetery. Just as I was about to return to Delhi, a friend in Australia sent me a newspaper clipping which made mention of the first Australian-born novelist, John Lang, who spent the last years of his life in Mussoorie and was known to have been buried here. There is still an unsolved mystery about Lang's manuscripts. He left his papers to his second wife, nee Margaret Watter, but neither they, nor any trace of her after his death, have ever been found.

John Lang was born in Sydney in 1816. His father, a young soldier turned merchant, died before his birth. His mother was Elizabeth Harris, born on Norfolk Island, the daughter of two convicts. Lang proved a brilliant Latin scholar at Sydney College, then went to England to study law. He was expelled from Cambridge for *Botany Bay Tricks*—believed to be the writing of the blasphemous litanies—but was admitted to the Society of the Middle Temple and called to the bar in 1841. He returned to Sydney shortly afterwards, but his convict connections stood in the way of his advancement, and it was only when he went to India that he began to lead a successful legal and literary life. *The Forger's Wife*—a robust tale of Australian outlaws—was published in England in 1855; *Botany Bay*—a collection of stories based on life in Sydney in the early years of the century—was written for Charles Dickens' magazine *Household Words* and published in 1859. The best of his books on India are *The Weatherbys* (1853) and *The Ex-Wife* (1859). These take a lightly satirical look at English social life in India, and are precursors of Kipling's stories of Simla society.

Lang practiced at the Bar in Calcutta, and represented the Rani of Jhansi in her legal battles against the East India Company. He did well both as a barrister and as a newspaper proprietor. But none of his manuscripts, and no portrait of him, have ever been discovered. When he died he left everything to his second wife, whom he married in Mussorie in 1861: but what happened to her after his death remains a mystery.

Although Lang's books are elusive, I decided that his grave should not be so hard to find, and set out in search of it on a crisp October morning. This is the best time of year in the hills, with the hillsides sprinkled with wild geranium and umbrella-fronds of lady's lace.

I take Camel's Back Road that leads round the northern and more forested face of Gun Hill, which is a rocky outcrop in the centre of the hill station. Gun Hill is so named because in Lang's time, it boasted a cannon which boomed out at noon each day. The gun was a mixed blessing. Once on a Sunday morning during service in the Anglican church of

St Thomas (built in 1834 and now beginning to crumble), one of Fisher's straw cannon balls shot through the open door, bounced off a pew, and landed in the lap of a stout lady who had been sleeping through the sermon. Fisher was finally relieved of his job, and the cannon was shifted to the municipal godowns where, for all I know, it may still be gathering rust.

Although Mussoorie's Camel's Back Road was not as high in social hierarchy as Scandal Point in Simla, it was, until the 1930s, almost exclusively a European preserve; and so was the cemetery, where most of the names on the tombstones are of Anglo-Saxon vintage. The graves occupy terraced slopes which face the snow-covered Nilkanth and Bandarpoonchh ranges.

I'm unable to enter at the gate which is securely padlocked and encircled by barbed wire, making the two large noticeboards—'No Trespassing' and 'Visitors Should Leave Their Dogs Behind'— seem rather unnecessary. I walk along the railing until I notice a small footpath leading off the verge. Climbing over the railings, I start down the path; but it is steep and slippery with pine needles, and I end by tobogganing down the slope into a thicket of myrtle.

Brushing dust, burrs and pine needles from my clothes, I stand up and survey the hillside, my eyes finally coming to rest on a small knoll where several bulky obelisks rise from the ground. Obelisks were all the rage in the late 19th century, and it is just possible that John Lang's grave will be among them.

The knoll does seem to be the oldest part of the cemetery; it is certainly the prettiest. The sunlight penetrating the gaps in the tall trees, plays chess on the gravestones, shifting slowly and thoughtfully across the worn old stones. The wind, like a hundred violins, plays perpetually in the topmost branches of the deodars. The only living thing in sight is an eagle, wheeling high overhead. The snows are just a great dazzle in the sky. This is a romantic spot, fit burial ground for adventurers and pioneers. Here are the graves of soldiers, merchants, evangelists. The largest of the graves belongs to Mr Henry Bohle, who died in 1852. The financial benefits accruing to the hill station from Bohle's Brewery (now a ruin) led to Mackinnon going one better by building a cart road for his produce, and this road formed the basis for the present motor road from Dehra to Mussoorie.

There are a number of Mackinnons buried here. But unless John Lang his window in a generous mood, the chances of my finding his grave here are rather remote. Only the more expensive gravestones with marble insets have retained their inscriptions. The sandstone graves are now just anonymous slabs. Over a hundred monsoons have worn away the lettering on many old trombs.

I'm still searching the knoll when I am hailed by a man holding a bundle of sticks in one hand and an axe in the other. He calls out to me in a belligerent tone:

'What are you doing here? And how did you get in?'

'I am looking for a grave,' I reply mildly.

'You may come across your own grave if you walk in here without permission!'

This must be the mali, who is both gardener and caretaker. I have been warned about him; a fierce man who has been to eject intruders at the point of a lathi. I am told he is short-sighted; andand, like a bear, which is also short-sighted, believes that there is no point in trying to identify an intruder until he has been finished off.

It is only when the mali comes closer, and finds that I look fairly respectable, that his bluster disappears.

'Some people come here to rob the graves,' he explains in an injured tone. 'And every time an arm or a head or a piece of marble goes,' he says, gesturing towards a decapitated angel, 'the Committee memsahibs take me to task for carelessness.'

'Well, I'll tell the memsahibs how vigilant you are. I am looking for an old grave. Over a hundred years old.'

'There are some old ones near my house,' he says, beginning to mellow. 'But you should look at the register, sahib. That will help you find your relative's grave.'

I am about to tell him that it is not a relative's grave, then decide not to as I do not want to raise his suspicions again. And it is pleasant to invent a relationship with another writer, a fellow Indo-Anglian, who lived, loved, died and was buried here over a hundred years ago.

'Who has the register?'

'The Garlah miss-sahib. She will tell you everything.'

'All right, I'll see her and come again tomorrow.'

'If you bring a chit from the miss-sahib, I can open the gate for you.'

I continue searching on my own for a while, to the evident unease of the male. Does he really think I shall make off with a headstone?

That evening I visit Miss Garlah. She is a tubby little

Anglo-Indian lady with a hearty manner and a strong constitution. Forty of her sixty years have been spent in Mussoorie.

'Did you have trouble with the mali?' she asks with apparent relish. Evidently she looks forward to getting complaints about him.

'He was a bit aggressive,' I say. 'He needs glasses to help him separate grave robbers from other people.'

'Well, he saw you climbing the railings, and that made him wonder what you were up to.'

'So he's been to you already?'

'Yes, he's very good. We keep him because he's so tough. The last man used to let in all sorts of people, including some hippies who thought the cemetery would be just the right place for smoking pot.'

When I tell her the object of my search, she says: 'Yes, I have a register. Give me the name and date of your author's death and we'll look him up.'

'John Lang, 1864.'

'Ah, that's going too far back. There must have been a register for those years, but if there was, it's long since lost. I can help you from 1910 onwards.'

I make no attempt to hide my disappointment. 'Nothing earlier? If only I had an idea of where the grave might be situated, I might be able to identify it.'

'Well, young man, I can only suggest that you keep hunting. Try the graves near the mali's house. I'll ask him to clean them up for you. You may be lucky. We do our best to maintain them because the British High Commission makes us a small grant towards their upkeep. But we're short-handed, and the heavy monsoon rains don't help.'

The next day I am back at the cemetery, determined to make one more attempt at finding John Lang's grave. I am leaving for Delhi in a day or two, and it may be months, perhaps, years, before I can return to Mussoorie.

This time I find the gate open. A small boy with little on goes skipping over the graves, like some mischievous cupid trying to resurrect dead lovers. His father, the mali, appears from behind a placid buffalo and gives me an elaborate salaam. Apparently Miss Garlah has already sent word of my coming.

The mali apologizes for the condition of some of the graves near his outhouse. His buffalo is tethered to a crumbling obelisk. A cow and calf are tied to a slanting stone cross. Several graves are half-buried under straw and offal. Others appear to have vanished into a small ploughed field which now contains mustard. The strangest sight of all is a memorial tablet, commemorating a certain Captain Jones of Her Majesty's 30th Foot, which lies flat on the gardener's tall and ornate hookah pipe.

The chances of finding John Lang's grave in this tumbled crumbling heap now seem remote. But the mali offers to help me in my search and he is so anxious to please that I am loath to disappoint him. He starts scraping the mud off partly obscured inscriptions and tells his small son, a merry little fellow with bright eyes and a disarming smile, to do the same. It is glorious day, but the wind is from behind the mali's house, and there is no escape from the odour of sour milk and cow dung. I came in search of the dead, only to find the living.

We find several graves dating from 1864 and earlier, but John Lang's is not one of them. I begin to harbour mean thoughts about his wife. If she could disappear so suddenly and mysteriously with his manuscripts, it is unlikely that she would have bothered to give him an expensive and permanent grave.

'There were a few on this northern slope, sahib,' says the mali after some time, 'but we had a landslide a few years ago and the graves went down the khud.'

This is enough to make me give up all hope. For all I know, John Lang's remains may well be at the foot of the mountain. My search becomes desultory, and I find myself muttering, 'What does it matter, anyway? If a writer's any god, his books will be his monument. What need have we of tombstones to commemorate our passage on earth?'

But all the same I am disappointed. And seeing my disappointment, the mali makes renewed efforts to clean up some of the graves near the cattle shed. He cannot understand my whim, or anyone's sentimentality over old graves, but he has warmed towards me, wants to please me and would be quite willing to chisel 'John Lang, died 1864' into any grave I choose, if it will make me happy.

Three weeks after leaving Mussoorie, I receive a letter from Miss Garlah, informing me that the old register had turned up and that John Lang had indeed been buried in the Mussoorie cemetery, on 'C' terrace.

On a subsequent visit I made my way to the spot and found the grave quite easily, under a covering of moss and ferns; shaded by the deodars, it was just a mound of earth and foliage. Prem and I cleared away a hundred years of detritus, and there on a plain stone slab was the simple inscription—'John Lang, Barrister at law. Died Landour, 1864, aged 47.'

RUSKIN BOND

The Himalaya Club

IT IS SOME eighteen years since* this institution was founded, at Mussoorie, one of the chief sanataria in the Himalaya mountains. Here all those who can obtain leave, and who can afford the additional expense, repair to escape the hot weather of the plains. The season begins about the end of April, and ends about the first week in October. The club is open to the members of the civil and military services, to the members of the bar, the clergy, and to such other private gentlemen as are on the Government House list, which signifies, 'in society.' The club-house is neither an expensive nor an elegant edifice, but it answers the purposes required of it. It has two large rooms, one on the ground-floor, and the other on the upper story. The lower room, which is some sixty feet long by twenty-five wide, is the dining-room, breakfast-room, and reception-room. The upper room is the reading and the ball-room. The club has also its billiard-room, which is built on the ledge of a precipice; and its stables, which would astonish most persons in Europe. No horses except those educated in India, would crawl into these holes cut out of the earth and rock.

Facing the side-door is a platform about forty yards long by fifteen feet wide; and from it, on a clear day, the eye

---

*John Lang wrote 'The Himalaya Club' in 1859.

commands one of the grandest scenes in the known world. In the distance are plainly visible the eternal snows; at your feet are a number of hills, covered with trees of luxuriant foliage. Amongst them is the rhododendron, which grows to an immense height and size, and is, when in bloom, literally covered with flowers. On every hill, on a level with the club, and within a mile of it, a house is to be seen, to which access would seem impossible. These houses are, for the most part, whitened without as well as within; and nothing can exceed in prettiness their aspect as they shine in the sun.

From the back of the club-house, from your bed-room windows (there are twenty-three sets of apartments) you have a view of Deyrah Dhoon. It appears about a mile off. It is seven miles distant. The plains that lie outstretched below the Simplon bear, in point of extent and beauty, to the Indian scene, nothing like the proportion which the comparatively pigmy Mont Blanc bears to the Dewalgiri. From an elevation of about seven thousand feet the eye embraces a plain containing millions of acres, intersected by broad streams to the left, and inclosed by a low belt of hills, called the Pass. The Dhoon, in various parts, is dotted with clumps of jungle, abounding with tigers, pheasants, and every species of game. In the broad tributaries to the Ganges and the Jumna, may be caught (with a fly) the mâhseer, the leviathan salmon. Beyond the Pass of which I have spoken, you see the plains of Hindoostan. While you are wrapped in a great coat, and are shivering with the cold, you may see the heat, and the steam it occasions. With us on the hills, the thermometer is at forty-five; with those poor fellows over there, it is at ninety-two degrees. We can scarcely keep ourselves warm, for the wind comes from the snowy range; they cannot breathe, except beneath a punkah. That steam is, as the crow flies, not more than forty miles from us.

We are all idlers at Mussoorie. We are all sick, or supposed to be so; or we have leave on private affairs. Some of us are up here for a month between musters. We are in the good graces of our colonel and our general—the general of our division, a very good old gentleman.

Let us go into the public room, and have breakfast; for it is half-past nine o'clock, and the bell has rung. There are not more than half a dozen at the table. These are the early risers who walk or ride round the Camel's Back every morning: the Camel's Back being a huge mountain, encircled about its middle by a good road. The majority of the club's members are asleep, and will defer breakfast until tiffin time—half-past two. At that hour the gathering will be great. How these early risers eat, to be sure! There is the major, who, if you believe him, has every complaint mentioned in 'Graham's Domestic Medicine,' has just devoured two thighs (grilled) of a turkey, and is now asking Captain Blossom's opinion of the Irish stew, while he is cutting into a pigeon-pie.

Let us now while away the morning. Let us call on some of the grass widows. There are lots of them here, civil and military. Let us go first to Mrs Merrydale, the wife of our old friend Charley, of the two hundredth and tenth regiment. Poor fellow! He could not get leave, and the doctors said another hot summer in the plains would be the death of his wife. They are seven hundred pounds in debt to the Agra bank, and are hard put to it to live and pay the monthly instalments of interest. Charley is only a lieutenant. What terrible infants are these little Merrydales! There is Lieutenant Maxwell's pony under the trees, and if these children had not shouted out, 'Mamma! Mamma! here is Captain Wall, Sahib!' I should have been informed that Mrs Merrydale was not at home, or was poorly, which I should have believed implicitly. (Maxwell, when a young ensign, was once engaged to be married to Julia Dacey, now Mrs Merrydale, but her parents would not hear of it, for some reason or other.) As it is, we must be admitted. We will not stay long. Mrs Merrydale is writing to her husband. Grass widows in the hills are always writing to their husbands, when you drop in upon them, and your presence is not actually delighted in. How beautiful she looks! now that the mountain breezes have chased from her cheeks the pallor which lately clung to them in the plains; and the fresh air has imparted to her spirits an elasticity, in lieu of that languor by which she was oppressed a fortnight ago.

Let us now go to Mrs Hastings. She is the wife of a civilian, who has a salary of fifteen hundred rupees (one hundred and fifty pounds) per mensem, and who is a man of fortune independent of his pay. Mrs Hastings has the best house in Mussoorie. She is surrounded by servants. She has no less than three Arab horses to ride. She is a great prude, is Mrs Hastings. She has no patience with married women who flirt. She thinks that the dogma—

When lovely women go astray,

Their stars are more in fault than they—is all nonsense.

Mrs Hastings has been a remarkably fine woman; she is now five-and-thirty, and still good looking, though disposed to *embonpoint*. She wearies one with her discourses on the duties of a wife. That simpering cornet, Stammersleigh, is announced, and we may bid her good morning.

The average rent for a furnished house is about five hundred rupees (fifty pounds) for the six months. Every house has its name. Yonder are Cocky Hall, Belvidere, Phoenix Lodge, the Cliffs, the Crags, the Vale, the Eagle's Nest, &c. The value of these properties ranges from five hundred to fifteen hundred pounds. The furniture is of the very plainest description, with one or two exceptions, and is manufactured chiefly at Bareilly, and carried here on men's shoulders the entire distance—ninety miles.

Where shall we go now, for it wants an hour to tiffin time? Oh! here comes a *janpan*! (a sort of sedan-chair carried by four hill men, dressed in loose black clothes, turned up with red, yellow, blue, green, or whatever colour the proprietor likes best). And in the *janpan* sits a lady—Mrs Apsley, a very pretty, good-tempered, and well-bred little woman. She is the grand-daughter of an English peer, and is very fond of quoting her aunts and her uncles. 'My aunt Lady Mary Culnerson,' 'my aunt the Countess of Tweedleford,' 'my uncle, Lord Charles Banbury Cross,' &c. But that is her only weakness, I believe; and, perhaps, it is ungenerous to allude to it. Her husband is in the Dragoons.

'Well, Mrs Apsley, whither art thou going? To pay visits?'

'No. I am going to Mrs Ludlam's to buy a new bonnet, and not before I want one, you will say.'

'May I accompany you?'

'Yes, and assist me in making a choice.'

There is not a cloud to be seen. The air is soft and balmy. The wild flowers are in full bloom, and the butterfly is on the wing. The grasshopper is singing his ceaseless song, and the bees are humming a chorus thereto.

We are now at Mrs Ludlam's. The *janpan* is placed upon the ground, and I assist Mrs Apsley to step from it.

Mrs Ludlam is the milliner and dressmaker of Upper India, and imports all her wares direct from London and Paris. Everybody in this part of the world knows Mrs Ludlam, and everybody likes her. She has by industry, honesty of purpose, and economy, amassed a little fortune; and has brought up a large family in the most respectable and unpretending style. Some people say that she sometimes can afford to sell a poor ensign's wife a bonnet, or a silk dress, at a price which hardly pays. What I have always admired in Mrs Ludlam is that she never importunes her customers to buy her goods; nor does she puff their quality.

The bonnet is bought; likewise a neck-scarf for Jack. And we are now returning: Mrs Apsley to her home, and I to the club. Mrs Apsley invites me to dine with them; but that is impossible. It is public night, and I have two guests. One of them is Jack, who does not belong to the club, because Mary does not wish it.

Mrs Apsley says she wants some pickles, and we must go into Ford's shop to purchase them. Ford sells everything; and he is a wine, beer, and spirit merchant. You may get anything at Ford's—guns, pistols, swords, whips, hats, clothes, tea, sugar, tobacco. What is this which Ford puts into my hand? A raffle paper! 'To be raffled for, a single-barrelled rifle, by Purdey. The property of a gentleman hard-up for money, and in great difficulties. Twenty-five chances at one gold mohur (one pound twelve shillings) each.'

'Yes, put my name down for a chance, Ford.'

'And Captain Apsley's, please,' says the lady.

After promising Mrs Apsley most faithfully that I will not keep Jack later than half-past twelve, and taking another look into those sweet eyes of hers, I gallop away as fast as the pony can carry me. I am late; there is scarcely a vacant place at the long table. We have no private tables. The same board shelters the nether limbs of all of us. We are all intimate friends, and know exactly each other's circumstances. What a clatter of knives and forks! And what a lively conversation! It alludes chiefly to the doings of the past night. Almost every other man has a nickname. To account for many of them would indeed be a difficult, if not a hopeless task.

'Dickey Brown! Glass of beer?'

'I am your man,' responds Major George, N. I. Fencibles.

At the other end of the table you hear the word 'Shiney' shouted out, and responded to by Lieutenant Fenwick of the Horse Artillery.

'Billy! Sherry?'

Adolphus Bruce of the Lancers lifts his glass with immense alacrity.

It is a curious characteristic of Indian society that very little outward respect is in private shown to seniority. I once heard an ensign of twenty years of age address a civilian of sixty in the following terms: 'Now then, old moonsiff, pass that claret, please.'

The tiffin over, a gool, or lighted ball of charcoal, is passed round the table in a silver augdan (fire-holder). Every man present lights a cigar, and in a few minutes there is a general move. Some retire to the billiard-room, others cluster round the fireplace; others pace the platform; and two sets go up-stairs into the reading-room to have a quiet rubber—from three till five. Those four men seated at the table near the window have the reputation of being the best players in India. The four at the other table know very little of the game of whist. Mark the difference! The one set never speak, except when the cards are being dealt. The other set are finding fault with one another during the progress of the hand. The good players are playing high. Gold mohur points—five gold mohurs on the rub—give and take five to two after the first game. And sometimes, at game and game, they bet an extra five. Tellwell and Long, who are playing against Bean and Fickle, have just lost a bumper—twenty-seven gold mohurs—a matter of forty-three pounds four shillings.

In the billiard-room, there is a match going on between four officers who are famed for their skill, judgment, and execution. Heavy bets are pending. How cautiously and how well they play! No wonder, when we consider the number of hours they practise, and that they play every day of their lives. That tall man, now about to strike, makes a revenue out of billiards. I shall be greatly mistaken if that man does not come to grief some day. He preys upon every youngster in every station he goes to with his regiment. He is a captain in the Native Infantry. His name is Tom Locke. He has scored forty-seven off the red ball. His confederate, Bunyan, knows full well that luck has little to do with his success. He, too, will come to grief before long. Your clever villains are invariably tripped up sooner or later, and ignominiously stripped of their commissions and positions in society.

It is five o'clock. Some thirty horses and as many ponies are saddled and bridled, and led up and down in the vicinity of the club. Everybody will be on the mall presently. The mall is a part of the road round the Camel's Back. It is a level of about half a mile long and twelve feet broad. A slight fence stands between the riders and a deep khud (precipice). To gallop along this road is nothing when you are accustomed to it; but at first it makes one very nervous even to witness it. Serious and fatal accidents have happened; but, considering all things, they have been far fewer than might have been expected.

The mall is crowded. Ladies and gentlemen on horseback, and ladies in *janpans*—the *janpanees* dressed in every variety of livery. Men in the French grey coats, trimmed with white serge, are carrying Mrs Hastings. Men in the brown clothes, trimmed with yellow serge, are carrying Mrs Merrydale. Jack Apsley's wife is mounted on her husband's second charger. 'Come along, Captain Wall,' she calls out to me, and goes off at a canter, which soon becomes a hard gallop. I follow her of course. Jack remains behind, to have a quiet chat with Mrs Flower, of his regiment; who thinks—and Jack agrees with her—that hard riding on the mall is a nuisance, and ought to be put a stop to. But, as we come back, we meet the hypocrite galloping with a Miss Pinkerton, a new importation, with whom—much to the amusement of his wife—he affects to be desperately in love. The mall, by the way, is a great place for flirtations.

Most steady-going people, like Mrs Flower, not only think hard riding on the mall a nuisance, but make it the theme of letters to the editors of the papers; and sometimes the editors will take the matter up, and write leading articles thereon, and pointedly allude to the fact—as did the late Sir C. J. Napier in a general order—that beggars on horseback usually ride in the opposite direction to heaven. But these letters and leaders rarely have the desired effect; for what can a man do when a pretty woman like Mrs Apsley says, 'Come along; let us have a gallop.'

Why are there so very many people on the mall this evening? A few evenings ago it was proposed at the club that a band should play twice a week. A paper was sent round at once, and every one subscribed a sum in accordance with his means. Next morning the required number of musicians was hunted up and engaged. Two cornets, two flutes, two violins, a clarionet, a fife, and several drums. It is the twenty-ninth of May—a day always celebrated in 'this great military camp,' as Lord Ellenborough described British India. At a given signal, the band strikes up 'God save the Queen.' We all flock round the band, which has taken up a position on a rock beetling over the road. The male portion of us raise our hats, and remain uncovered while the anthem is played. We are thousands of miles distant from our fatherland and our

Queen, but our hearts are as true and as loyal as though she were in the midst of us.

This is the first time that the Himalaya mountains have listened to the joyous sound of music. We have danced to music within doors; but never, until this day, have we heard a band in the open air in the Himalaya mountains. How wonderful is the effect! From valley to valley echo carries the sound, until at last it seems as though every mountain now had found a band.

Long after the strain has ceased with us, we can hear it penetrating into and reverberating amidst regions which the foot of man has never yet trodden, and probably will never tread. The sun has gone down, but his light is still with us.

Back to the club! Dinner is served. We sit down, seventy-five of us. The fare is excellent, and the champagne has been iced in the hail which fell the other night, during a storm. Jack Apsley is on my right, and I have thrice begged of him to remember that he must not stay later than half-past twelve; and he has thrice responded that Mary has given him an extension of leave until daylight. Jack and I were midshipmen together, some years ago, in a line-of-battle ship that went by the name of the *House of Correction*. And there is Wywell sitting opposite to us—Wywell who was in the frigate which belonged to our squadron—the squadron that went round the world, and buried the commodore, poor old Sir James! in Sydney churchyard. Fancy we three meeting again in the Himalaya mountains!

The cloth is removed, for the dinner is over. The president of the club—the gentleman who founded it—rises. He is a very little man of seventy years of age—fifty-three of which have been spent in India. He is far from feeble, and is in full possession of all his faculties. His voice is not loud, but it is very distinct, and pierces the ear.

They do not sit long after dinner at the club. It is only nine, and the members are already diminishing.

Some are off to the billiard-room, to smoke, drink brandy-and-water, and look on at the play. The whist parties are now at work, and seven men are engaged at brag. A few remain; and, drawing their chairs to the fireplace, form a ring and chat cosily.

Halloa! what is this? The club-house is heaving and pitching like a ship at anchor in a gale of wind. Some of us feel qualmish. It is a shock of an earthquake; and a very violent shock. It is now midnight. A thunderstorm is about to sweep over Mussoorie. Only look at that lurid forked lightning striking yonder hill, and listen to that thunder! While the storm lasts, the thunder will never for a second cease roaring; for, long before the sound of one peal has died away, it will be succeeded by another more awful. And now, look at the Dhoon! Those millions of acres are illuminated by incessant sheet lightning. How plainly we discern the trees and the streams in the Dhoon, and the outline of the pass which divides the Dhoon from the plains. What a glorious panorama! We can see the black clouds descending rapidly towards the Dhoon, and it is not until they near that level land that they discharge the heavy showers with which they are laden. What a luxury would this storm be to the inhabitants of the plains; but it does not extend beyond the

Dhoon. We shall hear the day after to-morrow that not a single drop of rain has fallen at Umballah, Meerut, or Saharunpore.

The party from the billiard-room has come up to have supper, now that the storm is over. They are rather noisy; but the card-players take no heed of them. They are too intent upon their play to be disturbed. Two or three of the brag party call for oyster-toast to be taken to the table, and they devour it savagely while the cards are dealt round, placing their lighted cheroots meanwhile on the edge of the table.

And now there is singing—comic and sentimental. 'Isle of Beauty' is followed by the 'Steam Leg,' the 'Steam Leg' by the 'Queen of the May,' the 'Queen of the May' by the facetious version of 'George Barnwell,' and so on. Jack Apsley—who has ascertained that dear Mary is quite safe, and not at all alarmed—is still here, and is now singing 'Rule, Britannia,' with an energy and enthusiasm which are at once both pleasing and ridiculous to behold. He has been a soldier for upwards of sixteen years; but the sailor still predominates in his nature; while his similes have invariably reference to matters connected with ships and the sea. He told me just now, that when he first joined his regiment, he felt as much out of his element as a live dolphin in a sentry-box, and he has just described his present colonel as a man who is as touchy as a boatswain's kitten. Apsley's Christian name is Francis, but he has always been called Jack, and always will be.

It is now broad daylight, and high time for a man on sick-leave to be in bed. How seedy and disreputable we all look, in our evening dresses and patent-leather boots. And observe this carnation in my button-hole—the gift of Mrs Apsley; she gave it to me on the mall. The glare of the lights, and the atmosphere of smoke in which I have been sitting part of the night, have robbed it of its freshness, its bloom, and perfume. I am sorry to say it is an emblem of most of us.

Go home, Apsley! Go home, reeking of tobacco-smoke and brandy-and-water—with your eyes like boiled gooseberries, your hair in frightful disorder—go home! You will probably meet upon the mall your three beautiful children, with their rosy faces all bloom, and their breath, when they press their glowing lips to those feverish cheeks of yours, will smell as incense, and make you ashamed of yourself. Go home, Jack. I will tiff with you to-day at half-past two.

~

Two young gentlemen were victimized last night at the brag party. The one, a lieutenant of the N. I. Buffs, lost six thousand rupees; the other, a lieutenant of the Foot Artillery, four thousand. The day after to-morrow, the first of the month, will be settling day. How are they to meet these debts of honour? They have nothing but their pay, and must borrow from the banks. That is easily managed. The money will be advanced to them on their own personal security, and that of two other officers in the service. They must also insure their lives. The premium and the interest together will make them forfeit fourteen per cent per annum on the sum advanced. The loan will be paid off in three years, by monthly instalments. The paymaster will receive an order from the bank secretary to deduct for the bank so much per mensem from their pay. For the next three years they will have to live very mildly indeed.

There were also two victims (both youngsters) to billiards. One lost three thousand rupees in bets, another two thousand five hundred by bad play. They too, will have to fly for assistance to the banks. Captains Locke and Bunyan won, between them, last night, one thousand four hundred pounds. There was but little execution done at whist. Not more than one hundred and fifty pounds changed hands. Those four men who play regularly together, and who never exceed their usual bets, have very little difference between them at the end of each month—not thirty pounds either way. This will not hurt them; for they have all good appointments, and have private property besides.

I find, on going to tiffin at Jack Apsley's, that Mrs Jack has heard all about the winnings and losings at the club. Some man went home and told his wife, and she has told everybody whom she has seen. In a short time the news will travel to head-quarters at Simlah, and out will come a general order on gambling, which general order will be read aloud at the Himalaya Club, with comments by the whole company— comments which will be received with shouts of laughter. Some youngsters will put the general order into verse, and send it to a newspaper. This done, the general order will be converted into pipe-lights. This is no doubt very sad; but I have no time to moralize. My duty is simply to paint the picture.

Mrs Apsley is not angry with her husband for staying up

till daylight. She thinks a little dissipation does him good; and it is but a very little that Jack indulges in, for he is a good husband and a good father. Jack has a severe headache, but he won't confess it. He says he never touched the champagne, and only drank two glasses of brandy and water. But who ever did touch the champagne, and who ever did drink any more than two glasses of brandy and water? Jack came home with his pockets filled with almonds, raisins, prunes, nutcrackers, and two liqueur glasses; but how they got there he has not the slightest idea—but I have. Wywell, from a sideboard, was filling his pockets all the while he was singing 'Rule, Britannia.'

'Mrs Apsley, I have some news for you.'

'What is it, Captain Wall?'

'The club gives a ball on the 7th of June.'

'You don't say so.'

'And what is more, a fancy ball.'

The tiffin is brought in. Mulligatawny soup and rice, cold lamb and mint sauce, sherry and beer. The Apsleys are very hospitable people; but Mary, who rules the household, never exceeds her means for the sake of making a display.

The soup and a glass of wine set Jack up; and he becomes quite chirpy. He proposes that he and I and Wywell shall go to the fancy ball as middies, and that Mary shall appear as Black-eyed Susan. Then, darting off at a tangent, he asks me if I remember when we were lying off Mount Edgecombe, just before sailing for South America? But he requires a little more stimulant, for the tears are glistening in his soft blue eyes when he alludes to the death of poor Noel, a middy whom we buried in the ocean a few days before we got to Rio. In a very maudlin way he narrates to his wife the many excellent qualities of poor Noel. She listens with great attention; but, observing that his spontaneous emotion is the result of the two over-night glasses of brandy—plus what he cannot remember drinking over-night—she suggests that Jack shall make some sherry cobbler. What a jewel of a woman art thou, Mrs Apsley! Several of the men who returned home, as Jack did, none the better for their potations, have been driven by their wives' reproaches to the club, where they are now drinking brandy and soda-water to excess; while here is your spouse as comfortable as a cricket on a hearth; and now that he confesses he was slightly screwed, you, with quiet tact, contradict his assertion.

For the next week the forthcoming fancy ball to be given by the club will be the chief topic of conversation amongst the visitors at Mussoorie. Mrs Ludlam is in immense demand. She knows the character that each lady will appear in; but it is useless to attempt to extract from her the slightest particle of information on that head. This ball will be worth seven hundred and fifty rupees to Mrs Ludlam.

Let us keep away from the club for a few days; for, after several officers have been victimized at play, their friends are apt to talk about the matter in an unpleasant manner. This frequently leads to a quarrel, which I dislike to witness.

Where shall we go? To the Dhoon. It is very hot there; but never mind. No great-coat, no fires, an hour hence; but the very lightest of garments and a punkah. The thermometer is at eighty-five degrees there. The Dhoon is not a healthy place in the summer. It must have been the bed of an enormous lake, or small inland sea. Its soil being alluvial, will produce anything: every kind of fruit, European and tropical. You may gather a peach and a plantain out of the same garden. Some of the hedges in this part of the world are singularly beautiful, composed of white and red cluster roses and sweetbriers. There is an excellent hotel in the Dhoon, where we are sure to meet people whom we know.

Sure enough, I find a party of five at the hotel; all club men, and intimate friends of mine. They, too, have come down to avoid being present on the first settling day; for if there should be any duelling, it is just possible that some of us might be asked to act as second.

We must dine off sucking-pig in the Dhoon. The residents at Mussoorie used to form their pig-parties in the Dhoon, just as the residents of London form their whitebait banquets at Greenwich. I once took a French gentleman, who was travelling in India, to one of these pig-parties, and he made a very humorous note of it in his book of travel, which he showed to me. Unlike most foreigners who travel in English dominions, he did not pick out and note down all the bad traits in our character; but gave us credit for all those excellent points which his experience of mankind in general enabled him to observe.

The Governor-General's body-guard is quartered just now in the Dhoon, and there is a Goorkha regiment here. The Dhoon will send some twenty couples to the fancy ball on the 7th. Every lady in the place has at this moment a Durzee (man tailor) employed in her back verandah dressmaking. We are admitted to the confidence of Mrs Plowville, who is going as Norma. And a very handsome Norma she will make; she being rather like Madame Grisi—and she knows it.

We return to the club on the 2nd of June. There has been a serious dispute, and a duel has been fought; but happily, no blood shed. The intelligence of the gambling at the club has reached the Commander-in-Chief at Simlah; and he has ordered that the remainder of the leave granted to Captains Locke and Bunyan be cancelled, and that those officers forthwith join their respective regiments. The victims also have been similarly treated; yet every one of these remanded officers came up here on medical certificate.

It is the morning of the 7th of June. The stewards of the ball are here, there, and everywhere, making arrangements. Several old hands, who hate and detest balls, and who voted against this ball, are walking about the public room, protesting that it is the greatest folly they ever heard of. And in their disgust they blackball two candidates for admission who are to be balloted for on the 10th instant. They complain that they can get no tiffin, no dinner, no anything. But the stewards only laugh at them.

The supper has been supplied by Monsieur Emille, the French restaurateur, and a very splendid supper it is. It is laid out in the dining-room. Emille is a great artist. He is not perhaps equal to Brazier—that great man whom Louis Philippe gave to his friend, Lord William Bentinck, when Lord William was going out to govern India—but Emille, nevertheless, would rank high even amongst the most skilful of cuisiniers in Europe.

It is a quarter past nine, and we of the club are ready to receive our guests. The ladies come in *janpans*; their husbands following them on horseback or on foot. It is a beautiful moonlight night. We are always obliged to wait upon the moon when we give a ball in Mussoorie. Before ten o'clock the room is crowded. There are present one hundred and thirty-six gentlemen, and seventy-five ladies. Of the former nine-tenths are soldiers, the remainder are civilians. Of the latter, seventy are married; the remaining five are spinsters.

Here we all are in every variety of costume—Turks, Greeks, Romans, Bavarian broom-girls, Medoras, Corsairs, Hamlets, Othellos, Tells, Charles the Seconds, and Quakers. Many have not come in fancy costume, but in their respective uniforms; and where do you see such a variety of uniforms as in an Indian ball-room? Where will you meet with so great a number of distinguished men? There is the old general: that empty sleeve tells a tale of the Battle of Waterloo. Beside him is a general in the Company's service, one who has recently received the thanks of his country. He has seen seventy, but there is no man in the room who could at this very time endure so great an amount of mental or bodily fatigue. That youngster to the right of the general is to be made a brevet-major and a C.B. as soon as he gets his company. He is a hero, though a mere boy. That pale-faced civilian is a man of great ability, and possesses administrative talents of the very highest order. Seated on an ottoman, talking to Mrs Hastings, is the famous Hawkins, of the Third Dragoons. Laughing in the side doorway is the renowned William Mumble. He is the *beau ideal* of a dashing soldier. Yonder is Major Starcross, whose gallantry in Affghanistan was the theme of admiration in Europe. And there is Colonel Bolt, of the Duke's Own. All of these men have been under very hot fire—the hottest that even Lord Hardinge could remember. All of them are decorated with medals and ribbons. Where will you see handsomer women than you frequently meet in a ball-room at Mussoorie or Simlah? Amongst those now assembled there are three who, at any court in Europe, would be conspicuous for their personal attractions—Mrs Merrydale, Mrs Plowville, and Mrs Banks. Mrs Apsley is a pretty little woman; but the three to whom I have alluded are beautiful.

The dancing has commenced, and will continue until four o'clock, with an interval of half-an-hour at supper-time. The second supper—the ladies being gone—will then commence, and a very noisy party it will be. Unrestrained by the presence of the fair sex, the majority of those who remain will drink and smoke in earnest, and the chances are, there will be several rows. Ensign Jenks, when the brandy and water inflames him, will ask young Blackstone, of the Civil Service, what he meant by coming up and talking to his partner during the last set of quadrilles. Blackstone will say, the lady beckoned to him. Jenks will say, 'It is a lie!' Blackstone will rise to assault Jenks. Two men will hold Blackstone down on his chair. The general will hear of this, for Captain Lovelass (who is himself almost inarticulate) has said to Jenks, 'Cossider self unarrest!' Jenks will have to join his regiment at Meerut, after receiving from the general a very severe reprimand.

While talking over the past ball, an archery meeting or a

picnic is sure to be suggested. It must originate at the club; without the countenance of the club, which is very jealous of its prerogative, no amusement can possibly be successful. A lady, the wife of a civilian, who prided herself on her husband's lofty position, had once the temerity to try the experiment, and actually sent round a proposal-paper in her own handwriting, and by one of her own servants. She failed of course. All the club people wrote the word 'seen' opposite to their names; but withheld the important word 'approved.' Even the tradespeople at Mussoorie acknowledge the supremacy of the Himalaya Club.

~

The season is over. The cold weather has commenced in the plains. It is the 5th of October, and everybody at Mussoorie is on the move—going down the hill, as it is called. Every house which was lately full is now empty, and will remain so till the coming April. The only exceptions will be the schools for young ladies and for little boys; the convent, the branch of the North-West Bank, and the Post-Office. Invalided officers who reside at the sanatarium during the summer will go down the hill, and winter in Deyrah Dhoon. In another month the mountains will be covered with snow, and it would be dangerous to walk out on these narrow roads, few of which are railed in.

Let us sum up the events of the season. Four young men were victimized—two at cards and two at billiards. Two duels were fought on the day after the ball. In one of these duels an officer fell dead. In another the offending party grievously wounded his antagonist. Four commissions were sacrificed in consequence of these encounters. There were two elopements. Mrs Merrydale went off with Lieutenant Maxwell, leaving her children under the care of the servants, until her husband came to take them away. Mrs Hastings, who used to bore us about the duties of a wife, carried off that silly boy Stammersleigh. These elopements led to two actions in H.M. Supreme Court of Calcutta, and seven of us (four in one case and three in the other) had to leave our regiments or appointments, and repair to the Supreme Court to give evidence. Some of us had to travel fourteen hundred miles in the month of May, the hottest month in India.

There was another very awkward circumstance connected with that season at Mussoorie. The reader knows that Captains Locke and Bunyan were ordered to join their regiments, the unexpired portion of their leave having been cancelled by order of his Excellency the Commander-in-Chief. In the hurry of his departure from the hills, Locke had left in the drawer of a table a letter from Bunyan, containing a proposal to victimize a certain officer—then in Mussoorie—in the same manner that they had victimized one Lord George Straw; namely, to get him to their rooms, and play at brag. Lord George Straw had lost to these worthies eighteen hundred pounds on one eventful night. The general opinion was, touching a very extraordinary fact connected with the play, that Lord George had been cheated. This letter from Bunyan to Locke was found by the servant of the officer who now occupied the apartments recently vacated by Locke. The servant handed it to his master, who, fancying that it was one of his own letters, began abstractedly to read it. Very soon, however, he discovered his mistake. But he had read sufficient to warrant his reading the whole, and he did so. A meeting of gentlemen at the club was called; and, before long, Locke and Bunyan left the army by sentence of a general court-martial. I have since heard that Locke lost his ill-gotten gains in Ireland, and became eventually a marker at a billiard-room; and that Bunyan, who also came to poverty, was seen driving a cab for hire in Oxford-street.

It behoves me, however, to inform the reader that, recently, the tone of Anglo-Indian society during the hot seasons is very much improved. Six or seven years ago there never was a season that did not end as unhappily as that which I have attempted to describe; but it is now four years since I heard of a duel in the Upper Provinces—upwards of four years since I heard of a victim to gambling, and nearly three since there was an elopement. It is true that the records of courts-martial still occasionally exhibit painful cases; but, if we compare the past with the present, we must admit that the change is very satisfactory. I do not attribute this altered state of things to the vigilance of commanding officers, or the determination of the commanders-in-chief to punish severely those who offend. It is due chiefly to the improved tone of society in England, from which country we get our habits and manners. The improvement in the tone of Indian society has been very gradual. Twenty years ago India was famous for its infamy. Ten years ago it was very bad. It is now tolerable. In ten years from this date, if not in less time, Indian society will be purged entirely of those evils which now prey upon it, and trials for drunkenness and other improper conduct will happen as rarely as in England. Year by year this communication between our fatherland and the upper part of India will become more speedy and less expensive; and thus will a greater number of officers be enabled to come home on furlough for a year or two. Nothing does an Indian officer so much good as a visit to Europe. When a man has once contracted bad habits in India, he cannot reform in India. To be cured he must be taken away for a while from the country. There have been instances of officers who have had strength of mind to alter their course of life without leaving the East; but those instances are very few.

The East India Company should do all in its power to encourage young officers to spend a certain time every seven years in Europe. Instead of six months' leave to the hills— which six months are spent in utter idleness, and too frequently in dissipation—give them nine months' leave to Europe. This would admit of their spending six months in England, or on the Continent, where they would improve their minds and mend their morals, as well as their constitutions.

The East India Company should also bring the Peninsular and Oriental Company to reasonable terms for the passage of officers to and from India. A lieutenant who wishes to come home, cannot at present get a passage from Calcutta to Southampton under one hundred and twenty pounds. So that he gives up more than four months' pay for being 'kept' thirty-six days on board of a steamer. Three pounds ten shillings per diem for food and transit!

Military Matters

'A COURT MARTIAL! Is it possible?' exclaimed my friend, on looking into the general order book, which was put before him on the breakfast-table. 'Well, I did not think it would come to that.'

'I did,' said the Major of the regiment, who was sitting opposite to him. 'For it strikes me that the chief is never so happy as when he is squabbling with the members of the courts, and publicly reprimanding them for their inconsistency, or whatever else may occur to him. This is the seventh court martial held in this station within the past two months, and with the exception of one case, the whole of them were unnecessary.'

I was tempted to ask who was to be tried.

'Two boys,' replied the Major, 'who thought proper to quarrel at the mess-table, and to make use of a certain little word, not altogether becoming gentlemen, if applied to one another. The Senior Captain, who was the senior officer present, very properly put them under arrest, and sent them to their quarters. Our Colonel, who is, I am very happy to say, extremely particular on this as well as on every other point that tends to preserve the tone and character of the regiment, wished these lads to receive from a higher authority than himself a severe reprimand. That authority was the General of the Division; and if the General of the Division had been Sir Joseph Thackwell, an officer of sound judgment, or any commander of Sir Joseph's stamp, all would have been well. But the Colonel, who has since found out the mistake that he made in not weighing the individual character of Sir Doodle, forwarded the case on to him through the Brigadier in the regular way, the young gentlemen meanwhile remaining under arrest. The Colonel also saw Sir Doodle privately, and pointed out to him, so far as he could make himself understood, that a severe reprimand was all that was required. Sir Doodle, however, did not view the matter in this light, and forwarded the proceedings to the Commander-in-Chief, at Simlah. After a fortnight's delay, during which time those two boys have been confined to their respective bungalows, the order has come down for a general court martial, to assemble and try them. This will involve a further imprisonment of some three or four weeks; for the chief is sure to find fault with the court's finding, and send back the proceedings for revision and reconsideration previous to confirming and approving of them.'

'And what do you suppose will be the upshot?' I asked.

'That the lads will be released, or ordered to return to their duty,' said the Major. 'Have you ever witnessed a military court martial?'

'No.'

'Then I would advise you to witness this.'

On the following day, a frightfully hot day, the

thermometer being at ninety-two, I accompanied my friend in his buggy to the mess-room of the regiment, where I beheld some five-and-twenty officers in full dress. All these officers were in some way or other connected with the trial; besides these there were present some five-and-thirty officers in red or blue jackets, but without their swords; these were spectators. It was altogether a very imposing scene; especially when the thirteen members took their seats around the table, the President in the centre, and the Deputy-Judge-Advocate of the Division opposite to him; the prisoners standing behind the chair of the Deputy-Judge-Advocate-General. The lads were now perfectly reconciled to each other, and as good friends as ever. Indeed, on the morning that followed their use of the one very objectionable little word, mutual apologies and expressions of regret passed between them; and, in so far as the settling of the quarrel between themselves was concerned, it was most judiciously and satisfactorily arranged by their respective friends.

The court having been duly sworn, and the charges read aloud by the Deputy-Judge-Advocate-General, the prisoners were called upon to plead. Both of them wished to plead guilty, and said so in a low tone to the Deputy-Judge-Advocate-General, who in an equally low tone of voice, said—

'No, don't do that; say 'Not guilty.''

'But look here, my dear fellow,' said one of the prisoners to that functionary, who was the prosecutor on the occasion; 'what's the use of denying it? We did make two fools of ourselves.'

'Yes; what's the use of wasting time?' said the other prisoner.

'If we plead guilty, there's an end of it, and the court can sentence us at once, and send the papers up to Simlah by to-night's post. I am sick of that cursed bungalow of mine, and want to have a change of air.'

'Well, do as you like,' said the Deputy-Judge-Advocate. 'But my advice is that you plead *Not* guilty, and then in your defence you can put forth whatever you please in extenuation, and mitigation of the punishment.'

'But here we are brought up for calling each other liars in a moment of passion, and if we say we did not call each other liars, we *are* liars.'

'And what is more, we are liars in cold blood,' urged one of the prisoners.

'Will you admit that you were drunk?' said the Deputy-Judge-Advocate-General.

'No,' they both called out. 'We were not strictly sober, perhaps. But where is it about being drunk? We didn't see that in the charge.'

'Yes, here it is, in the second instance of the second charge, 'having while in a state of intoxication at the mess-table of her Majesty's —— Regiment of Foot, on the night,' &c., &c.

'Oh! that's an infamous falsehood, you know. Who said that? Not Captain Stansfield, who put us under arrest? If he swears that he shall answer for it. Intoxicated! not a bit of it! Screwed, nothing more!' cried the young officer in a sort of stage whisper. 'On my honour, as an officer and a gentleman, nothing more.'

'These charges have come down from head-quarters,

having been prepared in the office of the Judge-Advocate-General.'

'Who is he? What's his name?' asked the prisoners.

'Colonel Birch,' was the reply.

'Then he shall give up his authority.'

'Well, plead *Not* guilty, and you will have it.'

'Very well, then, off she goes: 'Not guilty!' Fifty not guilties, if you like, on that point.'

While this little, but interesting, debate was pending between the prosecutor and the prisoners, the various members of the court were holding with each other a miscellaneous conversation, or otherwise amusing themselves.

Colonel Jackstone, of the Native Infantry (who was the president of the court martial, in virtue of the seniority of his rank), was talking to Colonel Colverly of the Dragoons, about some extraordinary ailment of his wife which required the constant administration of brandy and soda-water, in order to keep her alive. It was a low sinking fever, he said, from which she had suffered for the last six or seven years at intervals of three months; and it was always worse in the hot weather than at any other season of the year. Captain Bulstrade, of the Artillery, was talking to Major Wallchaffe, of the Light (Bengal) Cavalry, concerning a fly-trap which he had that morning invented; a ginger-beer or soda-water bottle half filled with soapsuds and the opening besmeared with honey or moistened sugar. Captain Dundriffe was recommending Captain Nolens to buy some beer which a native merchant had recently imported into the station. Lieutenant Blade, of the Dragoons, was playing at odd and even with his fingers, on honour, with Lieutenant Theston, of the same regiment; and, with a pretence of being ready to take notes of the proceedings of the court martial, each, pen in right hand, was keeping an account of the score. Blade used to boast of being the inventor of this simple game, but there were officers in India who declared that it owed its existence to a late Commander-in-Chief of the Forces, and who invented it at school when he had been shut up in a dark room (with another boy as fond of gambling as himself), as a punishment for card playing and other games of chance requiring light to see what was going on. Nothing could possibly be simpler than the game, and played as it was, on honour, nothing could be fairer. Blade lost thirty pounds on the first day of the court martial, but won the greater part of it back on the day following. Of course it would not do to play at this game with strangers or promiscuous acquaintances. Lieutenant Belterton of the regiment was making use of the pens, ink, and paper, by sketching the President and several others who had somewhat prominent noses; and young Lofter was trying to rival him in this amusement. My own friend was very busy writing; and, from the serious expression on his countenance, you might have fancied he was composing a sermon, or writing a letter of advice to a refractory son; he folded up the paper, and passed it round till at last it reached me. I opened it, and read as follows:—'We shall be here till four. Take the buggy and drive up to the bungalow, and tell the khitmutghur to bring down the ice-basket, also Mr Belterton's ice-basket, with a plentiful supply of soda-water from our mess; for they are rather short here, and can't stand conviction, and therefore he confirmed and approved the sentence, or rather, as he had done that already, he rejected the appeal.

'Did he appeal to the Horse Guards?' asked the President.

'No, he belonged to the Company's service.'

'Well, did he appeal to the Directors? They might have restored him. They have just restored a man, Bagin, who was cashiered two years ago for gross fraud and falsehood in several instances.'

'Yes, I know. Bagin was in my regiment. But Bagin has an uncle in the direction, besides a stepfather who would have had to support him and his family if his commission had not been restored to him. Burkett had no friends, and very lucky for him.'

'How do you mean?'

'He entered the service of a native prince, and, being a steady fellow and a clever fellow, he made a fortune in the course of nine years, and is now living at home on his fifteen hundred a year.'

'I know of another case,' said another member of the court, and he proceeded to detail the particulars. When he had finished, another member told of another case; and so this desultory narration of individual experiences went on for one-hour-and-a-half—the Deputy-Judge-Advocate, with his tongue protruding, writing away as methodically as possible. What he was writing I do not know; but I fancy he was taking down the 'heads' of the various cases that were quoted, in order that his Excellency the Commander-in-Chief might have the satisfaction of examining them. I was a heavy run upon them. Tell him also to bring several bottles of our Madeira, for theirs I do not like, and won't drink. It has not age, and has not travelled sufficiently. Cigars also. I am literally bathed in perspiration, and so I fancy are most of us at this end of the table, for the punkah is too far distant to admit of our receiving any benefit therefrom. This is an awful business.'

In compliance with the request contained in the above note, I left the Court, drove off as rapidly as possible, and communicated my friend's wishes to his servant, who immediately hastened to fulfil them. By the time I returned to the Court the first witness was under examination. Such a waste of time! Such a trial to the temper of all present! Instead of allowing the Senior Captain to state the facts— and he would have done so in less than three minutes—and then take them down on paper, each question was written on a slip of paper, and submitted to the President, by the Deputy-Judge-Advocate, who showed it to the officers sitting on either side of him, who nodded assent. The question was then read aloud to the witness:—

'Were you present on the night of the 10th of April, at the mess-table of her Majesty's —— Regiment of Foot?'

The Captain replied, 'I was.'

The question and answer were then copied into 'the book,' and the slip of paper on which the question was originally written was torn up. This occupied (for the Deputy-Judge-Advocate was not a rapid writer, and was apparently in no particular hurry, being a man of very equable temperament) eight minutes. The second question was put in precisely the same way, the same ceremonies having been gone through. The second question was:—

'Were the prisoners present on that occasion?'

'They were,' replied the Captain.

Again the copying process went on, slowly and methodically, and Blade, who was still playing odd and even, called out in a loud voice, to make it appear that he was giving up his mind entirely to the investigation:—

'What was the answer? I did not hear it distinctly; be so good as to request the witness to speak up.'

'He said, 'They were,' returned the Deputy-Judge-Advocate-General.

'Oh! 'They were,' repeated Blade; writing down a mark, signifying that he had just lost four rupees.

Twenty minutes had now elapsed, and the above was all that had been elicited from the first witness, who was seemingly as impatient as most of the members of the Court. The Deputy-Judge-Advocate-General, however, had patience enough for all present, and so had Blade, and his adversary at odd and even. My friend having scowled at Blade for putting his question, and thus prolonging the inquiry, that aggravating officer now periodically spoke to the Deputy-Judge-Advocate-General, who invariably put down his pen to answer him; just as if he could not possibly speak with that instrument in his hand. It was a quarter-past two when the examination in chief was concluded. It began at twelve precisely; so that two hours and fifteen minutes had been consumed in taking down the following, and no more:—

'I was present on the night in question, and placed the

prisoners under an arrest, for giving each other the lie in an offensive and ungentlemanlike manner. They were excited seemingly by the wine they had taken; but I cannot say that they were drunk.'

The Court then adjourned for half-an-hour to the mess-room, to take some refreshment—every one dripping, drenched. Then came the opening the fronts of the thick red cloth coats, and the imbibing of brandy and soda-water, iced beer, and other fluids, and sundry violent exclamations, that it was worse than the battle of Sobraon—more trying to the constitution. Every one then sat down to tiffin; and, having hastily devoured a few morsels, smoked cheroots.

'I say, Blade,' said the Senior Captain, 'what did you mean by wishing me to speak up? Surely you heard my answer?'

'Mean, my dear fellow? I meant nothing—or if I did, it was only to take a mild rise out of you. However, don't interrupt me just now, for I am thinking over a lot of questions I intend to put to you, when we get back into Court.'

'Questions? About what?'

'About drink! That's all I will tell you now. You don't suppose that I was born the son of a judge of the Queen's Bench for nothing, do you? If so, you are vastly mistaken. Is that your Madeira, or ours?'

'Ours.'

'Then just spill some into this glass. Ours is not good, certainly, but it would not do to say so before the Colonel. Ah!' sighed the lieutenant, after taking a draught: 'that is excellent! Yes. Drink is the topic on which I intend to walk into you, practically. And be very careful how you answer, or you will have the Commander-in-Chief down upon you with five-and-twenty notes of admiration at the end of every sentence of his general order; thirty-five notes of interrogation in the same; and every other word in italics, or capitals, in order to impress the matter of his decision firmly on our minds. 'Was the Court raving mad? Witness ought to be tried!!! folly! imbecility! childishness! The veriest schoolboy ought to know better! Deputy-Judge-Advocate ignorant of his duty!!! The President insane!!!! Confirmed, but not approved!!!'

'What are you making such a noise about, Blade?' inquired the Colonel of his regiment, good-naturedly.

'Nothing, Colonel,' said Blade. 'No noise. But here is a man who has the audacity, in our own mess-house, to asperse the character of our Madeira.' And, taking up the Senior Captain's own bottle, and holding it before the Senior Captain's face, he exclaimed,—looking at the Colonel, 'He positively refuses to taste it, even.'

'Nonsense,' said the cavalry Colonel, approaching them with a serious air, and with an empty glass in his hand. 'Nonsense! Do you really mean to say that our Madeira is not good—excellent?'

'No, Colonel,' said the Senior Captain of the Royal Infantry regiment.

'Taste it, and say what you think of it, Colonel,' said Blade, filling the Colonel's glass, which was held up to receive the liquid, with a willingness which imparted some mirth to the beholders. 'Taste it. There.'

'I have tasted it,' said the Colonel, 'and pronounce it to be the best I ever drank in my life, and, in my judgment, infinitely superior to that of any other mess.'

'So I say,' said Blade, filling his glass; 'but the misfortune is, he won't believe me.'

'Order a fresh bottle of our wine for him, Blade,' said the Colonel, 'and let him taste the top of it.'

'No, thank you, Colonel,' said the Senior Captain; 'I would rather not. Remember, I have to conclude my examination.'

'Ah, so you have,' said the Colonel, moving away. 'But take my word for it, that better Madeira than ours was never grown or bottled.'

When the Court resumed its sitting, I observed that some of the members of the Court became drowsy, and dropped off to sleep, opening one eye occasionally, for a second or two; others became fidgety, impetuous, and argumentative. The President inquired if the members of the Court would like to ask the witness any questions. Several responded in the affirmative, and began to write their questions on slips of paper. Blade, however, was the first to throw his slip across the table to the Deputy-Judge-Advocate-General, who, having read it, handed it across to the President, who showed it to the officers on either side of him, who nodded assent. The question was then handed back to the Deputy-Judge-Advocate-General, who proceeded to read it aloud.

'You have stated that the prisoners were under the influence of wine, but that they were not drunk. What do you mean?'

'I mean,' said the Senior Captain, 'that they—'

'Not so quick, please,' said the Deputy-Judge-Advocate-General. 'You mean that?—Yes—I am quite ready.'

'I mean,' said the witness, 'that though they had both been partaking freely of wine, they were not—'

'Freely of wine—don't be in a hurry,' said the Deputy-Judge-Advocate-General, repeating each word that he took down.

'Mind, he says "Freely,"' said Blade. '"Freely of wine." The word "freely" is important—very important. Have you got down the word freely?'

'Yes,' said the Deputy-Judge-Advocate-General, having put down his pen to ascertain the fact, and make it known to his interrogator.

'Very well,' said Blade. 'Then put the rest of the answer down, at your earliest convenience. I am in no particular hurry.'

'Well?' said the Deputy-Judge-Advocate-General to the witness—'they were not—not what?'

'Not drunk,' said the witness.

'There is nothing about drunkenness in the charges,' said the President; 'where are the charges?'

'Here, sir,' said the Deputy-Judge-Advocate-General. 'But, please let me write down your remark before we go any further.'

'What remark?' inquired the President.

'That there is nothing about drunkenness in the charges. According to the last general order by his Excellency the Commander-in-Chief, on the last court martial held in this station, everything that transpires should be recorded.' And the Deputy-Judge-Advocate-General then resumed his writing in the slowest and most provoking manner imaginable. Several of the audience walked out of the Court, and went into the room where the refreshments were. I followed them. We remained absent for more than ten minutes; but, when we came back, the Deputy-Judge-Advocate-General had not yet written up to the desired point, previous to going on with Blade's question. This at length accomplished, he looked at the President and said, 'Yes, sir?'

'There is nothing about drunkenness, and the prisoners are not charged with it,' said the President. 'The words, 'while in a state of intoxication,' are to all intents and purposes surplusage.'

'There I differ with you, sir,' said the Deputy-Judge-Advocate-General.

'So do I,' said Blade.

'Clear the Court!' cried the President; whereupon the audience, the prisoners, the witnesses—in fact, all save the members of the Court and the Deputy-Judge-Advocate-General, withdrew, whilst a discussion, which lasted for three-quarters of an hour was carried on, every member giving his opinion, and most of them speaking at the same time.

When we returned to the Court, after three-quarters of an hour's absence, the Senior Captain resumed his seat near the Deputy-Judge-Advocate-General. We were not informed of what had taken place. A pause of several minutes ensued, when Blade threw across the table another little slip on which was written a long sentence. The Deputy-Judge-

Advocate-General handed it to the President, who, on reading it, looked a good deal astonished, and shook his head, whereupon Blade, who was evidently bent on mischief, called out, 'We are all of that opinion at this end of the table.'

The President then handed Blade's written question to the officer who sat next to him on his right, and that officer passed it on to the next, the next to the next, and so on till it had been seen by every member of the Court. Some signified by a nod, some by a shake of the head, others by a shrug of the shoulders, what they thought about it; and as there seemed to be a difference of opinion, the Court was again cleared in order that the vote for or against might be taken. So once more we were driven into the mess-room to refresh ourselves and laugh over the absurdity of the whole proceeding. After waiting there for about five-and-thirty minutes, the Adjutant announced, in a loud voice, 'The Court is open!' and we returned to hear the President say that, as it was now nearly four o'clock, the Court must be adjourned— another absurdity in connexion with courts martial. After four o'clock, the Court must not sit, even if twenty minutes in excess of that hour would end the proceedings, and render another meeting unnecessary.

The Deputy-Judge-Advocate-General then locked up his papers in a box, placed it under his arm, bowed to the Court, walked off, called for his buggy, and drove home. The members of the Court, the prisoners, and the audience then dispersed, and retired to their respective bungalows; all very tired, and very glad of some repose. My friend, on taking off his coat, asked me to feel the weight of it, out of curiosity.

Saturated as it was, it must, including the epaulettes, have weighed some five-and-twenty pounds.

The next day at eleven the Court again met. The first thing that was done was to read the proceedings of the previous day. This duty was performed by the Deputy-Judge-Advocate-General, and, slowly as he read, it was over in twelve minutes, for I timed him. That is to say, it had taken four hours and a half to get through the real business of twelve minutes, or, giving a very liberal margin, the business of half-an-hour.

And now another very curious feature of an Indian court martial presented itself. The President asked the Deputy-Judge-Advocate-General if he had furnished the prisoners with a copy of the past day's proceedings. The Deputy-Judge-Advocate-General said:—

'No, the prisoners had not asked for a copy.'

The President said:—

'That does not signify. Did you tender them a copy?'

'No, sir.'

'Then you ought to have done so.'

The prisoners here said that they did not want a copy.

The President's answer to this innocent remark was, that whatever they had to say they must reserve till they were called upon for their defence.

Desirous of not provoking the animosity of the President, they bowed, and very respectfully thanked him for the suggestion. Whereupon the President, who was a terrible talker, and passionately fond of allusions to his own career in the army, mentioned a case within his own personal knowledge. It was a case that happened in Canada, and he had reason, he said, to remember it, because he was at the time on the staff of that distinguished officer, Sir James Kemp, and heard Sir James remark upon it. The Honourable Ernest Augustus Fitzblossom, a younger son of the Earl of Millflower, was tried for cheating at cards, was found guilty, and sentenced to be cashiered. This sentence was confirmed and approved by the General Commanding-in-Chief, and the Honourable Lieutenant went home. An appeal was made to the Horse Guards, and it came out that no copy of each day's proceedings had been tendered to the prisoner, and upon that ground the whole of the proceedings were declared by his Royal Highness the Duke of York to be null and void. He (the President) did not mean to offer any opinion on that case, but he merely quoted it, and being on Sir James's staff at the time, he had reason to remember, in order to show that such was the rule.

A Captain in the Bengal Cavalry said he knew of a case which occurred in this country (India) where the very reverse was held. The prisoner—a Lieutenant Burkett, of the Bengal Native Infantry—was tried for being drunk whilst on outpost duty. The trial lasted for seventeen days, for no less than thirty-eight witnesses—principally natives—were examined. The Lieutenant, at the close of the case for the prosecution, demanded a copy of the proceedings, in order to assist him in drawing up his defence. His demand was not complied with. He was convicted and dismissed the service. He appealed to the Commander-in-Chief, who ruled that a prisoner had no right whatever to a copy of the proceedings until after his

told afterwards that we, the audience, and the prisoners, ought not to have been allowed to remain in court during this narration of cases, and the anecdotes which the narrators wove into them; but I need scarcely say I was very glad that our presence had been overlooked; for if I had not seen and heard what took place, I should not certainly have believed, and therefore should not have dreamt of describing it. It was during this conversation that Blade won back from his adversary, at odd and even, the greater portion of the money he had lost on the previous day; nor that either Blade or his adversary failed to take a part in the conversation, for both of them would now and then ejaculate 'What an extraordinary case!' 'Did you ever!' 'No, never!' 'It seems impossible!' 'Cashiered him?' 'Shameful!' 'Who could have been the chairman of the Court of Directors?' 'A Dissenter, I'll be bound!'

'Well, sir,' said the Deputy-Judge-Advocate-General to the President, when he had finished his writing, 'what shall we do? Shall we adjourn the Court until a copy of yesterday's proceedings is made, and given to the prisoners?'

'No doubt,' said the President; 'that is the only way in which the error can be repaired. But a copy must be delivered to each of them.'

'But had we better not take the opinion of the Court on the subject?' suggested the Deputy-Judge-Advocate-General.

'By all means,' conceded the President; 'but in that case, the Court must be cleared, while the votes are taken.'

'Clear the Court!' cried the Adjutant; and out we all marched again, into the mess-room, where more cheroots were smoked, and more weak brandy-and-water imbibed.

The third day came, and the Court re-assembled. The Deputy-Judge-Advocate-General read over the entire proceedings, beginning from the very beginning, the swearing of the members, up to the adjournment of the Court, and the reasons for such adjournment. Here another discussion or conversation ensued, as to whether it was necessary to read more than the last day's proceedings. The Deputy-Judge-Advocate-General said he was quite right. The President thought otherwise. All the other members of the Court spoke on the subject, many of them at the same time. Blade and his adversary also gave their opinions, the former for, and the latter opposed to the view taken by the President. As this was a point that must be cleared up, insomuch as the decision that might be come to would regulate the future proceedings in this respect, the Court was again 'cleared,' and we again marched into the room where the refreshments were to be had. In half-an-hour's time we were re-admitted. But it was not until the following day (for members are not allowed, in short, they are bound by oath not to divulge what may be decided when the doors are closed), that we learnt the Deputy-Judge-Advocate-General had carried his point, and that a sort of parody of that old nursery story, about 'the fire began to burn the stick, the stick began to beat the dog, the dog began to bite the pig,' was the proper way to open the proceedings of each day during a protracted trial by general court-martial!

So curiously is human nature constituted, that I, in common with the rest of the audience, began, after the fifth day, to like the business, and to watch its various twistings

and turnings with great interest. The mess-house, at which
the Court was held, became a favourite lounge for almost
everybody in the station; and it was curious to hear the bets
that were made with reference to the probable 'finding,' and
the sentence. The trial lasted over thirteen days, inclusive of
two Sundays which intervened; and the proceedings were
then forwarded to Simlah, where they remained for a fortnight
awaiting the decision of the Commander-in-Chief, who, in
fulfilment of Blade's prophecy, certainly did put forth 'a
snorter of a General Order,' and as full as it could be of italics,
capitals, and notes of exclamation and interrogation. His
Excellency 'walked into' the President, and recommended
him to study some catechism of the Law of Courts Martial,
such a book as children might understand. His Excellency
further remarked that the Senior Captain (the principal
witness), or any man wearing a sword, ought to be ashamed
of admitting that he was unable to define the various stages
of intoxication; and that he was astounded to find that the
Court in general should have paid so little attention to the
admirable reasoning, on this point, of a junior member whose
intelligence appeared to have enlisted no sympathy. (This
had reference to Blade.) His Excellency went on to say, that
he had never himself been drunk in the whole course of his
long life, and to that fact he attributed his position; that if the
Court had done its duty it would have cashiered the prisoners;
that a 'severe reprimand which the Court awarded was a
mockery which stunk in the nostrils,' and that the prisoners
were to be released from arrest and return to their duty
without receiving it. But the Chief did not end here. He went

on to say, that he would maintain the discipline of the British army in the East, in all ranks, or else he would know the reason why. And being, I fancy, in some difficulty as to what to use, in the case (whether marks of admiration or interrogation), he emphasized the last word of this culminating and very relevant sentence thus:—

'WHY?!!!'

It was a matter of grave doubt whether the determination, thus expressed, to uphold discipline in the army, was in any way assisted by such general orders as those fired off from the pen of the ardent Commander-in-Chief; the more especially as such general orders were copied into the newspapers, and were read by (or listened to while others were reading aloud,) every non-commissioned officer and private in Upper India, Native and European. Three weeks after the promulgation of the general order just alluded to, a trooper in the Dragoons having been talked to seriously by the captain of the troop, for some irregular conduct, thus unburthened himself:—

'You! What do I care for what YOU say? You are one of those infernal fools whom the Commander-in-Chief pitched into the other day for BEING a fool.' And as the peroration of this speech consisted of the dashing off of the speaker's cap, and hurling it into the captain's face, the man was tried, convicted, and sentenced to be transported for life.

If it be inquired by the reader whether the above description of a Court Martial in India is a fair specimen of what usually transpires at these tribunals, I reply, emphatically, 'Yes,' and I make the assertion after having watched the proceedings of no fewer than eighteen Courts Martial during my sojourn in the East Indies.

Four officers who had obtained six months' leave of absence, and who had rented between them a furnished house at Simlah, were about to proceed there. I was tempted to accompany them. We left Umballah at sunset in palkees, and at seven o'clock on the following morning arrived at the foot of the hills, at a place called Kalka, where there is an hotel. Having breakfasted, we commenced the ascent on ponyback, and in the course of an hour and a-half arrived at Kussowlie, where a regiment of her Majesty's Foot was quartered. Here we rested for a brief while, and then pursued our journey. Strange to say, although the climate is superb, and the scenery grand beyond description, the men (so I was told) preferred the plains, regarding them—to use their own words—'less like a prison than the hills.' From Kussowlie we pushed on to Sirée, which is about half way between Simlah and Kalka. Here there is a bungalow, at which we dined on the everlasting 'grilled fowl,' hard-boiled eggs, and unleavened bread. Some friends at Simlah, who had been written to previously, had sent five horses to meet us; so that, when we resumed our journey, we were mounted on fresh cattle. All along the road the scenery is extremely picturesque and beautiful; but, in point of grandeur, it does not, in my opinion, equal that of the Alps.

It was nearly dark when we arrived at our destination and entered the house, where we found everything ready for our reception; the servants had been sent on a day or two in advance of us.

It is a long and fatiguing ride, forty miles in the sun, albeit there is generally a light breeze to modify the heat; and we were all disposed to retire to rest. But we were unable to do so. The gentlemen who had sent the horses to meet us, as soon as they were informed of our arrival, came to see us, and, what was more, to take us to a subscription ball, which was to take place that night at the Assembly Rooms. It was useless to plead weariness. We were compelled to go.

The society of Simlah, though composed of the same elements, differs very much from the society of Mussoorie. The presence of the Commander-in-Chief, or the Governor-General, and sometimes both (as was the case when I was at Simlah), imposes a restraint on the visitors to this sanitarium. The younger men are less disposed to run riot, and incur the risk of having their leave cancelled, and themselves sent down to the plains. A ball, therefore, at Simlah differs from a ball at Mussoorie. It is so much more sedate. More than one half of those who prefer Simlah to Mussoorie, do so in the hope of prepossessing one or other of the Great Authorities, by being brought into contact with them, and thus obtain staff employ or promotion; and very amusing is it to look on at a public entertainment and witness the feelings of jealousy and of envy that swell the breasts of the various candidates for notice and favour. Nor are the little artifices that are resorted to unworthy of observation and a smile. At this ball there was a lady, the wife of a civilian (a sad fool), who had a great facility in taking likenesses, and she had drawn the Governor-General in every possible attitude, both on foot and on horseback. These clever and admirably-executed sketches were laid upon a table in the ball-room, and excited very general admiration; and it was very soon 'buzzed about' who was the artist. The wife of another civilian, however, maliciously neutralized the effect these sketches would probably have had, by falsely saying, loud enough for his Lordship to hear, 'Ah! she said she would do the trick with her pencil!' The consequence was, that when the lady's husband begged his Lordship would accept this collection of portraits, as well as a few sketches of the house inhabited by the Great Man, his Lordship,—as delicately and as gracefully as the circumstances would admit of—'declined them with many thanks;' just as though they had been so many unsuitable contributions to some popular periodical. The wife of a military officer, however, was rather more fortunate. She, too, had a great talent for drawing, and had taken an excellent likeness in water colours of the Commander-in-Chief's favourite charger—the charger that had carried the old Chief through his battles; and as the lady begged that the Chief would accept the picture, he did so, and the next *Gazette* made known that Captain Cloughcough was a Major of Brigade. By the way, this was an excellent appointment, for the office required no sort of ability, and Cloughcough had none; he was, moreover, a most disagreeable person in his regiment, and constantly quarrelling with his brother officers, who were delighted to get rid of him. To chronicle *all* the seductive little arts which were resorted to on that night, to effect a desired end, would half fill a volume. But I cannot omit the following: it struck me as so *extremely* ingenious. There was a lady, the wife of a young civilian, who had two very pretty little children—a boy and a girl. Of these children, the Governor-General took great notice, and, whenever he saw their mother, made inquiries touching 'the little pets,' as he was won't to speak of them. On the night of that ball, his Lordship did so. The lady replied that they were quite well; but that the doctor had said their return to the plains would be fatal to them, and that they must be sent to England.

'Then you had better take the doctor's advice,' said the Governor-General.

'But, alas! my Lord,' said the lady, 'we have not the means. My husband's pay is only 700 rupees a month, and we are, unfortunately, very much in debt.'

'That's a bad job,' said my Lord.

'Yes,' sighed the lady; 'it is a very painful reflection—the idea of losing one's little dears. But what is to be done? I dread the coming of the 15th of October, when my husband's leave will expire, more than I dread my own death.'

'Could you not remain up here with them through the winter?'

'And be absent from my husband, my Lord? Besides, two establishments on 700 rupees a month!'

'That is true.'

'If we could *send* them to England under the care of some friend, we would do so, before the hot weather sets in. But we cannot afford it. Or if my husband had an appointment in some healthy station, out of the plains, then they might be spared to us. The thought of the beautiful roses on their cheeks just now leaving them, and their dear little faces becoming pale and sallow, and their little limbs shrinking till they are almost skeletons—it makes my very heart bleed!' (And the pretty and ingenious little lady took her kerchief, raised it to her eyes, and suppressed something like one of Mrs Alfred Mellon's stage sobs, which went, straight as an arrow, to the Governor-General's sensitive heart.) 'If,' she continued, 'my husband were a favourite with the Secretary; but he is not—for he is too independent to crave—then the case would be very different.'

'The Secretary!' exclaimed the Governor-General, 'what has he to do with it?'

(The lady had aroused his Lordship's sympathy, and now she had touched his pride, and inflamed his vanity.)

'I thought he had all to do with it, my Lord.'

'You shall see that he has *not*,' said the Governor-General. 'Be comforted, my dear madam, and come to the refreshment room.' His Lordship gave her his arm, and led her away from the couch on which they had been conversing.

This 'children's dodge,' as it was called, was eminently successful. The lady's husband was appointed superintendent of one of the most delightful hill stations in India, on a salary of 1200 rupees (120*l.*) per mensem.

The ball over, at half-past two in the morning we returned to our house, where I was disgusted to hear that a leopard had carried off out of the verandah a favourite dog of mine. It is no easy matter to keep a dog in Simlah, except in the house. The leopards are always on the look-out for them, and will often carry them off in your very sight, while you are riding or walking along the road.

The great business at Simlah, as at Mussoorie, is devising the means of amusement, or rather of varying the amusements so as to render them less irksome than they would otherwise become. Cards and billiards are the principal pastimes; and, now and then, pic-nic and excursion parties are got up; and, once or twice a month, private theatricals are resorted to.

Invitations to dinner-parties and evening-parties are plentiful enough; but to men who go to Simlah without wives and families, and who don't intend to marry in the East, these reunions are a bore rather, after a brief while, and such men prefer dining under their own roofs. There was an hotel at Simlah, kept by a Frenchman, who provided a *table d'hôte* every day at seven o'clock. This used to be very well attended; for, generally speaking, better fare was to be got there than anywhere else. By the way, the host had once been an officer in the French army, and was rather a touchy man. On one occasion an officer complained of the character of some dish on the table, and was challenged to 'fight with either sword or pistol.' This challenge was declined; but the officer said he would have no objection to an encounter, provided the weapons were cold legs of mutton.

There is an enormous mountain at Simlah, and around its base there is a good macadamized road, some fifteen feet wide. This is the favourite ride of the visitors, and every fine afternoon some sixty gentlemen, and nearly as many ladies, may be seen upon it taking the fresh air.

Simlah is a much more expensive place to spend the summer at than Mussoorie, in consequence of its great distance from the plains, whence almost every article of food and all descriptions of 'stores' are carried on men's shoulders. The mutton of the hill sheep is not equal to Welsh mutton; but when properly kept and dressed, it is very good eating.

The hill cattle also afford tolerable beef; but the joints are very small. House-rent at Simlah is also much dearer. The furnished abode, for which we paid 100*l.* for the season, we could have got at Mussoorie for 60*l.* The same may be said of articles of clothing and of merchandize. The majority of the European shopkeepers (there were only five or six) appeared to be doing a good business; but I question whether they made money. They have to give, in most cases, very long credit, pay high rates of interest to the banks for money, and high rents for the extensive premises they are obliged to occupy, to say nothing of having to live as all English people must live in India. The hotel did not pay the proprietor, notwithstanding his house was generally full of people, and his charges were seemingly exorbitant.

There was no club at Simlah when I was there; but, since then, one was established. Its existence, however, was very brief. The fact is, people in India very soon grow tired of a thing; and, what is even worse, you will find that when a large number of persons, who have really nothing to do but amuse themselves, very frequently meet, they wrangle, quarrel, split into small coteries, and become on very bad terms with each other. How the old Himalaya Club at Mussoorie has existed so long, is miraculous. A club in India is not like a club in England, where scores of the members are unknown to each other, even by name, and possibly do not meet more than once in a month.

Some of the views at Simlah are magnificent; and from several points may be seen, in the far distance, the river Sutlej, stealing its way through the mountains. The water has the appearance, when the sun is shining upon it, of a narrow stream of quicksilver. Some of the hills are literally covered with rhododendron trees, fifty or sixty feet high, and when they are all in full bloom the effect may be easily imagined.

To Jutsy, some five or six miles from Simlah, and where one of the Goorkha battalions was always stationed, I have already alluded. There are but two or three bungalows there, and they are occupied by the officers of the battalion.

The season that I spent at Simlah was a very pleasant one, and notwithstanding it was enlivened by several exciting incidents—to wit, a duel, a police affair, a court martial, and an elopement—I was very glad when it was over, and we could return to the plains.

The Himalayas

I [HAD MET] a German Baron and a French gentleman [in Agra, who] like myself, were, travelling in search of the picturesque, and with a view to become acquainted with Oriental character from personal observation.

While staying with my friend at Barnapore, I received a letter from the former, proposing that we should meet on a certain day at Mussoorie, in the Himalaya mountains, and travel into the interior together. I agreed with all my heart; and my friend, the assistant magistrate, was tempted to apply for six weeks' leave, in order that he might accompany us.

Let me describe these foreign gentlemen. They were respectively about my own age—thirty-two—had seen a great deal of the world, and of the society at every court and capital in Europe. They were both possessed of considerable abilities, and of the most enviable dispositions; always good-natured and good-tempered; patient and cheerful under those innumerable little difficulties that almost invariably beset a wanderer in the East, or, in fact, a wanderer in any part of the world. They had, moreover, a keen sense of humour; and, each in his own peculiar way, could relate a story, or an incident in his life, in such a manner as to make it wonderfully mirth-provoking. They were men of refined understanding and of very refined manners: take them all in all, they were the most charming companions I ever encountered. They were utterly devoid of vulgar nationalities—of any enthusiastic admiration of their own fatherlands, and would just as soon ridicule the foibles peculiar to their own countries, respectively, as the foibles of a man of any other country. My friend the assistant magistrate was also a desirable companion. He, too, was a good-tempered, good-humoured being, with a keen sense of humour, and some wit. He had read a great deal of late years, in that out-of-the-way station to which he had been appointed, and he had profited by his reading.

It was beginning to be very hot in the plains, and my friend and myself were not a little glad when we found ourselves on the road to a colder clime. We drove as far as Deobund in the buggy; and, at three p.m. threw ourselves into our *palanquins* (palkees), bound for Deyhra Dhoon at the foot of the hills; at which place we arrived at about nine o'clock on the following morning, and were deposited—both of us fast asleep—in the verandah of the hotel, kept by a Mr William Johns, who had been formerly a professional jockey in the North-West Provinces of India.

So much has been written of Deyhra Dhoon and Mussoorie, that even a brief sketch of these places would be unwarranted in this narrative.

As soon as we arrived at Mussoorie we began to collect coolies (hill-men), to carry our baggage and stores. We required in all about one hundred and fifty for the expedition, and by the time that we had got these people together, and made arrangements with them, and the guides whom we required, and had laid in our stock of provisions, &c., the foreign gentlemen joined us, and expressed their readiness to start at any given moment. We lingered, however, for two days, in order that they might take some rest, and make the acquaintance of the gentlemen at the club, who, at the instance of my friend, had made them as well as myself honorary members of the institution.

On the third morning, in the front of the club-house, our marching establishment was collected, and the one hundred and fifty men of whom it was composed were laden with the baggage and stores. There were tents, the poles thereto belonging, camp tables, chairs, beds, bedding, leather boxes of every kind, containing our clothing, &c., deal chests, containing all sorts of provisions, dozens of cases of wine—port, sherry, claret—beer, ducks, fowls, geese, guns (rifles and others), umbrellas, great-coats, &c., &c., &c. Having seen this train fairly off, we, the four of us, followed shortly after on foot, and overtook them at the Landour Hill, a mountain about nine thousand feet above the level of the sea. We were all in high spirits—including my friend the assistant magistrate—notwithstanding he put on his lady love's cloak as soon as we were out of sight of the club, and began to quote in a melancholy but very loud voice, which reverberated through the valleys on either side of us, those glorious lines of the poet Thomson:—

'There is a power
Unseen, that rules th' illimitable world—

That guides its motions, from the brightest
Star to least dust of this sin-tainted mould;
While man, who madly deems himself the lord
Of all, is nought but weakness and dependence.
This sacred truth, by sure experience taught,
Thou must have learnt, when wandering all alone:
Each bird, each insect flitting through the sky,
Was more sufficient for itself than *thou!*'

Our first halting-place was about nine miles from Mussoorie. It was a flat piece of ground, some distance down the southern face of the peak over which the road wound. The place was called Sowcowlee, and here and there were to be seen a few patches of cultivation and a cowshed. Our course lay in the direction of Almorah, another Hill Sanatarium for the English in India. The tents pitched, and all made snug and comfortable, we threw ourselves down upon our beds, not to sleep, but to take some rest after a long walk. Meanwhile our servants busied themselves in preparing the dinner, for which the exercise and the change of air had given us all a keen appetite.

'Well!' exclaimed my friend (whom in future we will call Mr West), raising to his lips a bumper of claret, and quoting from the Sentimental Journey, 'the Bourbon is not such a bad fellow, after all.'

Neither the Frenchman nor the German understood the allusion; but when it was explained they relished it amazingly. We were rather a temperate party; and after the second bottle of wine was emptied, we caused the glasses to be removed from our small table, and a green cloth spread over it. We then began to play at whist—a game of which we were all equally fond; and, what was of great consequence, we were all equal as players. We did not gamble exactly; but the stakes were sufficiently high to make either side attend very carefully to the game. The whist over, we each took a tumbler of warm drink, and turned in for the night, and slept, as the reader may imagine, very soundly.

On the following morning, at sunrise, we were awakened, and informed that upon a hill opposite to our encampment there were several large deer. We arose, and went in pursuit of them. After dodging them for some time we came within range, and each of us, selecting his animal, fired. One shot only took effect, and that was from the Baron's rifle. During our ramble we discovered that there were plenty of pheasants in the locality, and so we agreed to remain for the day, and, after breakfast, see what we could do amongst them. Under the circumstances we should have been compelled to halt, for, as is usual on such occasions, our servants had forgotten several little matters essential for our comfort, if not necessary for our journey, namely, the pickles and the sauces, the corkscrew, the instrument for opening the hermetically sealed tins containing lobsters, oysters, and preserved soups. Amongst other things that had been left behind was the Baron's guitar, and without it he could not, or would not, sing any of his thousand and one famous German songs. And such a sweet voice as he had! So, while we were amongst the pheasants, five coolies were on their way back to Mussoorie, to bring up the missing articles above enumerated.

By two o'clock, we had bagged eleven noble birds, and

returned to our encampment, sufficiently hungry to enjoy the refreshments which the Khansamah (butler), who was a great artist in his way, had prepared for us. Our repast concluded, we had our camp bedsteads brought into the open air, and threw ourselves down on them.

Holding his cigar between the thumb and forefinger of his left hand, the Baron thus went off:—

'Who can explain the inscrutable mystery of presentiments? Who can fathom the secret inclinations of the human heart? Who can lift the veil of sympathy? Who can unravel the web of magnetic natures? Who can fully comprehend that link which unites the corporeal with the spiritual world? Who can explain that terrible symbol which pervades so many of our dreams? The sweet anxiety that seizes us when listening to some wonderful tale; the voluptuous shiver which agitates our frame, the indefinite yearning which fills the heart and the soul. All this is a guarantee that some invisible chain links our world with another. Let no one condemn as idle nonsense that which our shallow reason may refuse to accept. Can the most acute understanding explain, or even comprehend, its own growth; or even the growth and colouring of a mere flower? Is not Nature herself a perfect mystery unto the minds of thinking men?'

'What is the matter, Baron?' asked the Frenchman. 'Have you a nightmare in this broad daylight?'

'No, no,' returned the Baron, with good-natured impetuosity. 'It is not so. I wish to tell you something—a little story, if you will listen.'

'Pray go on,' we (his three companions) cried out, simultaneously.

'Some ten or twelve years ago,' the Baron proceeded, 'I was travelling from Munich to Berlin. Tired by the continual rumbling of my carriage, I resolved upon taking a day's rest at Augsburg. It was the day of All Souls. The autumnal sun was shining brightly, and a large procession went its way towards the cemetery, a mile distant from the town. Wherefore, I know not; but I was instinctively led to join this procession. On arriving at the cemetery we found it, comparatively, crowded. All the graves were decked with flowers and sprigs of young cypress, and near every stone there sat or knelt, at least, one mourner. Tears of love and regret wetted the sacred earth. In a singularly agitated frame of mind, I wandered through the cemetery. The recollection of departed friends, and of dear ones far away, made me sad, unhappy, miserable. And I could not help thinking that if I had been then entombed, no friendly hand would on that day have deposited a wreath or a flower upon my grave, no beloved eye shed a tear of sorrow, no faithful heart sent up to Heaven a fervent prayer for the eternal rest of my soul. Haunted by such gloomy thoughts, I wandered on, and at last came to a newly-made grave. An hour previously had been buried in that spot a young girl of seventeen years of age. The parents and the lover of the girl stood weeping near her grave, and her young friends adorned the mound with freshly gathered flowers. In a fit of profound melancholy, I bent down, mechanically picked up a half-opened rose-bud, and walked on. Approaching the gate of the cemetery, with the intention of returning to my hotel, my eyes fell upon a tablet upon which were engraved the following words:—'Respect the property of the Dead. Flowers are the property of the Dead.' These simple words made a very great impression on my already excited mind: and glancing, involuntarily, at the rose-bud which I still held in my hand, my heart smote me for having carried it away from the girl's grave. I was on the point of returning to re-deposit the flower, when an indescribably false shame prevented my doing so, and I left the cemetery with the rose in my hand. On returning to my hotel, I put it in a glass of water, and placed it on a small table near the head of my bed, upon which I threw myself, and soon fell into that state which all of you must have experienced: a state in which the senses hover between sleep and wakefulness, as though undecided which to choose. Suddenly my apartment was filled by a bright but soft light, without my being able to perceive whence it came. Be it known that I had extinguished my candle. Ere long, the door of my room was opened; and in glided, noiselessly, a pale spectral figure, clad in a white robe, and wearing a garland of flowers. It was the figure of a young girl, and the face was angelic. With motionless eyes and outstretched hand she approached my couch, and in plaintive voice asked me: 'Why hast thou robbed the Dead? Why hast thou taken that flower which a faithful lover threw upon my last resting-place on earth?' Seemingly my pulses ceased to beat, and I could scarcely breathe. The phantom then stretched forth the left hand, and took the rose out of the glass; and with the right hand she beckoned to me, saying: 'Come! Come, and give back the property of the Dead. Respect the property of the Dead. Come! Follow me!' In vain I tried to resist. I arose, and followed the figure out of the room and into the deserted streets. It was not dark; for the moon was at her full and shining brightly. Onward stalked the figure, I followed her towards the cemetery. We arrived at the gate. She touched it. It opened noiselessly. We entered. She led me to the grave—the grave from which I had taken the flower. With trembling hand I received from hers the rose, and placed it on the very spot whence I had removed it. And then—'

Here the Baron paused—and relighted his cigar.

'Well—and then?' we all asked.

'Then,' replied the Baron, 'I awoke—that is to say, if I had ever been asleep. And looking in the tumbler in which I had placed the rose, I discovered that it was gone.'

'The chambermaid, possibly; or the waiter, who may have entered your apartment for orders, may have seen, admired, and carried it away while you were slumbering,' suggested the lively Frenchman; 'and a very lucky fellow you were, not to have missed your watch and your purse at the same time and place.'

'No,' said the Baron, shaking his head.

'Perhaps,' said Mr West, 'you had taken more wine than usual?'

'No,' was the reply. 'The truth is that the story I have related to you was written by that great Austrian wit and satirist, Saphir. It was one of his earlier compositions, which, strange to say, were all of a very melancholy cast. Saphir, however, to this day asserts that his story of 'The Death Rose' is a fact, and that it happened to himself.'

One by one, we dropped off to sleep, and slept for about an hour and a-half. On awakening, the Frenchman, West, and myself, almost simultaneously exclaimed, 'Confound your Death Rose, Baron!' for the truth was that the story had taken possession of our senses, while we were asleep.

'I thought it would,' said the Baron laughing. 'Everybody dreams of the Death Rose after I have told the story. But, ah! See in the distance! Here are the coolies returning! I can make out my guitar-box on the head of one man. Ah! to-night we will sing plenty of songs!'

And in the evening the Baron sang for several hours (we could have listened to him all night) some of the most sentimental, and some of the most humorous songs that I had ever heard. Fortunately I knew enough of German to appreciate them; and my friend, Mr West, was equally fortunate. As for the Frenchman he understood and spoke—albeit very imperfectly—every language current in Europe. On that night we retired before twelve, for we had agreed to rise and proceed early on the morrow.

In pursuance of such agreement, as soon as the day dawned we struck our tents, packed up our traps, loaded the coolies, and set out for a place called Demooltee, distant some fourteen or fifteen miles. The road, which had been very, very seldom travelled over by Europeans, was a narrow and bad road, winding round and leading over lofty peaks, some ten or eleven thousand feet above the level of the sea. Above us and below us we frequently saw herds of Ghooral and other deer; but as we could not, or would not rather, have stayed to pick up any that we might kill, we suffered them to graze on, and preserved our ammunition. By the way we saw an animal which none of as had ever seen before—an animal called the Seron. It is a species of chamois, but larger and stronger. Its colour was reddish, and it had a quantity of stiff, short hair on the neck, which gave it the appearance of a hogged mane. The native guides told us that it was a very shy animal, and only to be found where there was a great quantity of wood. The scenery of this part, in March, was exceedingly beautiful and varied. At times we had a good view of Mussoorie and the surrounding country. At other times we moved through vast forests of pine, and woods of oak, rhododendron, and other magnificent trees. In the midst of one of these woods our halting-place was situated, a large grassy flat, bounded on either side by a deep and steep precipice, while in every direction the surrounding mountains, which locked us in, were covered thickly with trees.

'What fools men are,' exclaimed the Baron, whilst the servants were unpacking, 'to huddle themselves together in old countries when lands like these remain uncultivated and unenjoyed! And what fools are those travellers who go, year after year, gazing on comparatively paltry mountains and lakes which the eyes of the vulgar of all nations have beheld, when such fresh and gorgeous scenery as this may be looked at! Travelling in Switzerland and Italy—bah!'

'But, my dear Baron,' said the Frenchman, 'you forget that the Peninsular and Oriental Company demand four pounds a day for conveying you from England to India, in consequence, they say, of the dearness of coals.'

'Ah! well,' laughed the Baron, opening with his own hand

a bottle of hock, and emptying the contents into a silver tankard, 'if you regard the matter in an economical point of view, you at once cut short my argument and my sentiment. Egad! what grapes could be grown on yonder hill, in that warm valley! What wine could be grown there! I will come out to this country with a few German peasants. I will have vineyards. I will make a fortune so colossal that Rothschild, when he is in difficulties, will have to write to me. Yes, I will. The thing is to be done, and I will do it.'

'But you forget,' said Mr West, 'that you are now some twelve or thirteen hundred miles from the nearest sea-port, Calcutta, and that there would be some little difficulty in transmitting the produce to Europe.'

'Europe! Europe! Why do you talk of Europe? Does not British India contain enough of Europeans to make a market? This bottle of good wine which we are going to drink costs twelve shillings in this country. I could grow it, make it, and sell it for one shilling a bottle! Ah! you may laugh; but I tell you this is the fact. I am a proprietor of vineyards, and do not speak at random like a schoolboy, or an enthusiast. The natives of the country would soon learn that art—for an art it is—of wine-making; and, as for the soil, it is superb. Yes! Grow wine, which would do your soldiers good. Generous wine, instead of that blood-drying, brain-consuming, soul-destroying arrack—your horrible grogs, and your bile-making beers.'

'But we have no roads, Baron.'

'True! But is there a scarcity of labour in India? Are pickaxes, shovels, spades, saws, and gunpowder to blast rocks, so expensive that a government cannot procure them? Roads! My good sir, only a few years ago there was no road over the Splügen! The time was when you had no road from Calcutta to Benares. You have no roads! Well, make them. The wine and the tea that you grow will more than pay for them, as well as remunerate the growers.'

'The tea?' asked Mr West.

'Yes, the tea, I said!' returned the Baron. 'You have discovered that you can grow tea in the lower range of these mountains, and you do grow it in small quantities; now why not, having made the experiment, grow it in *large* quantities? I would say to Mr Chinaman, 'I thank you very much, but I do not want any more of your tea. You are insolent, overbearing, and insulting in your dealings with me, and now you may drink your own tea, and I will drink *my* own tea; and, if you like, you may stir yours with your own pigtail. We will bring China into our own dominions, for God has given to this climate and to this soil the same properties as your soil and climate possess.' I do not say it, as you know, with any sort of intention to offend, but the result of my experience leads me to believe that the government of this country is, in all matters (save annexation), as slow as the government of the Dutch was in by-gone days. There is a listlessness and a languor about its movements; a want of everything in the shape of society and enterprise, and seemingly such an earnest desire to discourage the efforts of those who would in reality develop the resources of India, that I am astonished any man unconnected with the services should persevere in the attempt to make a living in the Eastern British dominions.'

'I quite agree with you,' said Mr West, 'especially as regards that portion of your remarks which relates to the obstacles thrown in the way of enterprising Englishmen. I have been a member of the Civil Service for nearly ten years, and have always been impressed with the idea that the policy of the government in respect to settlers in India, was and is a very erroneous policy.'

The conversation here was brought abruptly to a close by the approach of one of the guides, who, in a very confidential manner, imparted to us that there was a kakur (a barking deer) grazing on a crag not far from the encampment. So we seized our guns, went in pursuit, and were fortunate enough to kill the animal. His bark resembles exactly that of a Skye-terrier when very much excited. On our return to the encampment we encountered a huge bear, and succeeded in killing and carrying him to the door of our tent, where the natives skinned him and deprived him of his fat, which they boiled down and used in the lamps instead of oil. And very brightly did it burn; but the aroma was not a peculiarly pleasant one. I am afraid to say how much grease was taken from this enormous bear; but I know that I am speaking within bounds when I assert it was in excess of two gallons and a half.

We dined at dusk, and then, as usual, betook ourselves to whist, but so cold did it become shortly after dark, that we were forced to put on our great coats, notwithstanding there was an enormous wood fire in front and at the back of our tent. These fires had been lighted to serve another purpose beyond that of giving warmth—namely, to scare away the leopards which abounded in that locality. It was a very picturesque scene; the white tents standing out in relief from the dark wood, lighted up by the fires, and here and there groups of coolies wrapped up in blankets, and sitting as closely as possible to the blaze.

At daylight on the following morning our march was recommenced. We had a distance of ten miles to travel before we could reach the next halting-place, named Kanah Tall. During this march we did not go out of our way for game, but only took such as chanced to cross our path. All we killed was ghooral, (which we did not stop to look at even) and two braces of partridges of very peculiar plumage. They were remarkably handsome birds, with a red mark round the eye and down each side of the neck, olive-coloured feathers on their backs, and their wings and breasts covered with white-and-red spots. We could not fail to admire the beauty of the flowers which flourished in this locality. The ground on either side of the narrow and wild road was literally covered with violets, dog-roses, and a lily of the valley, and other little decorations of the earth, of which I know not the name. Throughout the whole march the scene was truly fairy-like. Kanah Tall was only five thousand feet above the level of the sea, and therefore very much warmer than our last halting-place. Of this we were by no means sorry, not only for our own sakes, but for the sakes of our personal servants, who had never before travelled out of the plains. Here, at Kanah Tall, we found the English holly growing. Botanists may tell me what they please about this holly of the Himalayas bearing a distinctive character; but I say it was the English holly—the same sort of holly that I saw last Christmas in almost every house in London and in the country.

Here, at Kanah Tall, we shot no less than seven elks. These deer are very plentiful hereabouts, and do a great deal of damage to the crops of the poor villagers at harvest time. Ghooral and kakur also abound here. We were so tired on the evening that we stopped at Kanah Tall that we could not sit up to play at whist! We actually fell asleep over our second rubber, and by general consent threw our cards upon the table and sought our beds.

The next day, at three p.m., we arrived at a place called Jullinghee, ten miles distant from Kanah Tall. Jullinghee is a large village situated on the right bank of the Bhagaruttee, a stream that flows direct from Gungootrie, and is in consequence one of the most sacred streams that compose the mighty and holy Ganges. We were encamped beneath a clump of apricot and walnut trees, but it was frightfully hot; for we were now not more than a couple of thousand feet above the level of the sea. The woods, however, were exceedingly beautiful and diversified. Not only were there apricot, walnut, rhododendrons, oaks, hollies, and other trees of the higher altitudes, but also the tamarind, the fig-peepul, the pomegranate, and others of the plains. At this village we procured some honey, which is taken from its makers in a very singular manner.

The bees build in cavities in the walls of the houses, which are closed within by a moveable board, and are only entered by the bees, by a small aperture from without. When the owners of the houses want honey they darken the interior of the house, and removing the board, which forms the back part of the hive, extract as much as they require. The bees during this process fly out into the light to discover their enemies, who then close the back part of the hive, and remain safely within doors until the wrath of the bees has subsided.

In the evening we took a walk in the village of Jullinghee, which appeared to be rich and populous, but very dirty. Our arrival had caused a great stir, and there was a large concourse of people near our tents to look at us. A short distance from the village were the ruins of several houses which once formed a separate hamlet, but which had been deserted for fear of a ghost which was said to haunt it. The same effect of superstition is by no means uncommon in the plains of India. There is a very curious instance in the Meerut district. A village had long been deserted under the idea that it was haunted by a fakir. The settlement officer, however, with much difficulty prevailed upon a neighbouring Zemindar to farm the land at something like a nominal revenue. Shortly afterwards the Zemindar presented himself to the settlement officer, and represented that he had been very ill, and that the visitation was ascribed by his friends and by himself to his impiety in interfering with haunted lands. The settlement officer, however, talked to him and insisted on his keeping his engagements, and once more did he venture to brave the ghost. So complete was his success that the village shortly became one of the most flourishing in the district, and the very relatives who had been foremost in reproaching the Zemindar for his impiety, brought a suit against him in one of the local courts, to recover a share of his large profits!

On the day following we marched to a place called Teree, a large straggling village, situated on a plain of some extent, at the junction of the Billung and Bhagaruttee rivers. A regular hot wind was blowing here, and our tents were unbearable; so we threw ourselves beneath the shade of a huge tree which grew on the banks of the Billung, and which served also as a shelter for a party from Srinugger, who were celebrating the marriage festival of a Bunneah (corn-merchant) of some twenty-two years of age, with a young lady of eight. The little damsel was on the ground, and did ample justice to the marriage dinner, which consisted of rice, butter, sweetmeats, and a goat roasted whole—a goat which had been decapitated by one blow, and cooked without any sort of preparation beyond the removal of the entrails; it was not even skinned. Portions of this feast were distributed on plantain leaves to each guest by the Brahmins, who officiated as cooks and waiters.

Teree is the residence of a Rajah, named Soodersain Saha, whose family, before the Goorkha invasion, ruled over the provinces of Gurhwal and Sirmoor, and indeed over the whole hill country as far as Simlah, and from the snowy range to the plains. Expelled by the Goorkhas, he sought refuge with the British: and after defeating the Goorkhas, was replaced by us in the greater part of his territories; a part of them we retained as the price of our assistance, namely, a portion of Gurhwal, the whole of Deyhra Dhoon, and a part of the Terai. And we hold Landour and Mussoorie from him at a nominal annual rent. The Rajah is extremely civil to Europeans, and the moment he heard of our arrival he sent a deputation to wait upon us. The deputation brought with them a variety of presents, consisting of milk, sweetmeats, dried flour, dried fruits, and a couple of goats. The deputation gave us to understand that it would afford the Rajah very great pleasure to make our personal acquaintance; and we were just on the point of starting for his Highness's abode, when his arrival was unexpectedly announced to us. At Srinugger, in a portion of the country we took from him, is situated the family palace, a handsome and substantial building. This is rather a sore point with the old Rajah, and as he considers the more modern abode which he now inhabits beneath his dignity, he prefers going to see any one with whom he is desirous of having an interview.

Having caused chairs to be placed in the front of our tents, we advanced to meet the Rajah, who, dismounting from a large Cabul horse, joined us, shook hands with us very cordially, and remained with us for upwards of an hour. He was a very small and rather an old man; active and intelligent. He talked to us about the Goorkha war, of which he had been a spectator in the British camp; and he was very eloquent on Punjab politics, and greatly praised Lena Singh, whom he described as 'very far in advance of any of his countrymen in point of humanity, civilization, and prudence.' The little man told us, amongst other things, that he was thinking of having an iron suspension-bridge over the Bhagaruttee, but that he could not find an engineer; and that his applications to the Government, although he was ready to defray every expense, had not met with any reply. The present bridge is a sling or swing, and constructed in the following manner.

Two lines of coir rope, each consisting of a number of smaller ropes, are suspended from the rocks on either side of the stream, and apart from each other about four feet. From these ropes depend, at intervals of about two feet, smaller lines or ropes about three or four feet deep. These support slight wooden ladders, the ends of which are lashed firmly to one another. The whole affair has a very frail appearance, and at first it requires no small amount of nerve to step from ring to ring of the ladder, over that roaring torrent beneath.

Of course this bridge is only passable by men. Cattle and mules swim across the river much higher up, where the torrent is not so rapid.

We asked the Rajah where he had got his idea of an iron suspension bridge, and he replied: 'From a picture-book which was given to me by a gentleman who was out on a shooting excursion some years ago in these hills.'

We stayed two days at Teree, and, despite the heat, enjoyed ourselves amazingly. Our next encampment ground was at a place called Pon, a march of eleven miles. Our route at first lay along the south bank of the Billung river, and then up a deep glen at the foot of a mountain, whose summit was some five thousand feet above the level of the ocean. The monotony of this day's journey was broken by meeting with another marriage party, some of whom carried parasols of evidently Chinese manufacture, and made out of painted paper. We shot also several green pigeons—a very different bird from the green pigeons of the plains, and much better eating. By-the-by we also met a pilgrim and his wife on their way to Gungootrie, the source of the Ganges: both of them were painted and bedaubed after the most grotesque fashion. The Frenchman took a sketch of this couple, and I have heard that it now adorns an album in the possession of the Empress of the French.

Our next march was to a place called Tekowlee, where we halted beneath the shade of some large trees, and near the banks of a clear stream of water. On one side of the stream there grew a quantity of wild mint, some of which we gathered and cooled, preparatory to using it for 'cup.' There is a moderate-sized village near Tekowlee, and a Gosains' house or monastery, which is inhabited by a large number of this sect: we visited, and entered into conversation with them. The building was composed of a large square court-yard, surrounded by a range of two-storied barracks, or rather cells, the lower story of which is protected by a verandah. The place was full of men, women, and children: the Gosains being the only monastic order who are permitted by their tenets to marry.

We had been out sixteen days before we reached Loba, near to which place the Commissioner of Kumaon resides during the rains and the autumn. His bungalow is built upon the spur of a hill of considerable length, and there is a good quantity of flat ground in the vicinity. Not far from the bungalow is an old fort, a Goorkha stronghold, which commanded the pass leading to Almorah. It is chiefly celebrated, however, as the place where Moorcroft and Hearsey were discovered on their return from the Munsarowar lake, whither they had gone disguised as Bairagis; and so well had they sustained their characters, that they would have returned undetected, had not a rumour of their attempt reached the ears of the authorities and excited their vigilance. They were harshly treated for some days, but eventually released on a promise that they would return direct, and without delay, to the British territories.

The Commissioner was not at the bungalow when we arrived. Mr West, however, knew him sufficiently well to warrant our taking possession of it for the day. After a residence for some time in tents, a house is a very agreeable change.

On leaving Loba we came upon the Pilgrim road, constructed by a former Commissioner of Kumaon to facilitate the progress of the pilgrims to the sacred places within the British Himalayas. It was a very humane project, for many of the unfortunate pilgrims used formerly— overcome by the difficulties of the route—to lie down and perish by the way-side. Of these pilgrims we met swarms— hundreds, if not thousands—and with some we occasionally stopped to converse.

Our encamping ground, at which we arrived at four in the afternoon, was a short distance from a village called Guniah. Our tents were pitched beneath a clump of trees, and close to a clear stream called the Ram Gunga, in which we caught a quantity of fish with a casting-net. There are some mines between Loba and Kumaon, but we did not go out of our way to visit them. Here an accident happened to the Baron. He sprained his ankle and could not walk; so the next morning we put him into a Dandi, and he was carried along the road by four of the coolies.

A Dandi is a pole, upon which is hung by its two ends, which are gathered together, a piece of cloth or canvas, open in the centre. This forms a hollow seat, not a particularly comfortable one, until you get accustomed to it, when the motion is rather pleasurable than otherwise. During this day's march we shot a quantity of black partridge, a hill fox, a deer, and a wild dog of enormous size.

On the third day after leaving Loba we sighted our (then) destination—the town of Almorah. On nearing the place we came upon a hill to the right, which bears the name of Brown's Hill; so called after an officer of the 31st Native Infantry, who, in the Goorkha war, volunteered to take it with his company, though it had a stockade on the top which was obstinately defended. And he did take it, after a very severe loss. A monument is erected on this hill to the memory of those who fell in the engagement. A little further on is a large tree now used as a gallows. This tree was the scene of a well-remembered occurrence, just after the above-mentioned battle. A Goorkha, shot through the leg, had fallen here. The fighting over, a British officer was standing over him, and giving directions to a party of Sepoys to have him taken to the hospital; when, raising himself with his left hand, with his right he cut the officer down with his kookeree—a deadly weapon with which the little Goorkhas now chop up the rebels.

Apropos of a kookeree in the hands of a Goorkha, I must relate a little matter which I now know to be a fact, but which I could scarcely credit when it was first told to me. A party of Goorkhas—say fifteen or twenty—will proceed to a jungle in which they know there is a huge tiger. They will surround the jungle, form a circle, and closing in gradually, hem in the ferocious beast. Every man will then drop down on the right knee, as soldiers do forming a square, and, kookeree in hand, wait for the spring of the tiger, who becomes somewhat bewildered and anxious to make his escape. After moving about for a brief while in this den, of which the bars are human beings (about five feet high), and glaring first at one and then at another, he lashes himself into a fury and makes his spring: then the nearest Goorkha delivers a blow with his kookeree which divides the tiger's skull. Wonderful as this feat is, I once saw at Jutog, near Simlah, a sight that struck me as even more wonderful. A Goorkha battalion was (and now is) quartered at Jutog. There was a festival at which the Goorkhas sacrifice an ox. The adjutant of the battalion asked me if I should like to witness the ceremony; as it was something new to me, I replied in the affirmative, and we walked to the parade ground, where the whole regiment, in undress, was assembled, and surrounding the victim and the executioner. The ox was forced to kneel, and by the side of him knelt the little Goorkha, armed with the kookeree, which is nothing more than a huge curved knife, but very heavy, and as sharp as a razor. At a given signal he struck the ox immediately behind the hump over the shoulder, peculiar to all Indian cattle; and the body was divided into two parts. He had, with a single blow, gone though the ox just as completely and as cleanly as a butcher with his hatchet would remove a chop from a loin of mutton. They are a very odd race of people, those little Goorkhas; wonderfully honest even among themselves; light-hearted almost to childishness; capable of enduring any amount of toil; obedient and respectful, without cringing to, fawning on, or flattering their superior, the white man. The great blot upon their characters is their frightful jealousy of their wives. Woe betide the woman who gives her Goorkha husband the faintest reason to suspect her of infidelity! He at once takes the law and the kookeree into his own hands, and slays both the wife and her (real or supposed) gallant. I am glad to say this is not a frequent occurrence, though it does happen now and then. As a body, the Goorkha women are as virtuous as their husbands are honest and brave.

The Commissioner of Kumaon received us at Almorah, his head-quarters, with great cordiality and kindness, and offered us rooms in his house. This offer we declined, inasmuch as our party consisted of four, and his house was not a large one. Besides, he had other visitors who were putting up at his bungalow. We accepted, however, his invitation to dine, and on our way rode through the town, which is considered the best in the British hill possessions. Bishop Heber writes that Almorah reminds him of Chester. It consists of one street about a mile and a half long, and about sixty feet wide, paved with large slabs of slate, and closed at either end by a gate. One half of the town is much higher than the other, and the street is divided in the middle by a low flight of steps on which the ponies pass up and down with extraordinary self-possession. The houses are small, but neat and whitewashed. They all consist of two or more stories. The lower ones are shaded by wooden verandahs more or less carved. At one end of the town is the old Goorkha fort; at the other end Fort Moira, a small English fortification, near to which were the Sepoy lines. A neat little church has just been erected at Almorah. The people of the place are all fair-complexioned, and some of the children as white as those born of European parents.

Returning

AT ALMORAH I parted company with my foreign friends. They intended crossing the mountains—the snowy range— to pay a visit to Kanawur. This was a journey for which I had not much inclination; besides I was doubtful whether I could breathe at an elevation of eighteen thousand feet above the level of the sea. As it was, several of the coolies died of cold and the rarity of the atmosphere. In fact, both of my friends themselves had, as they informed me afterwards, a very narrow escape. On several occasions they were compelled to huddle themselves amongst the coolies in their tent, and the sheep which they were taking with them for food were kept alive for the sake of the warmth they could impart in the canvas abode. The grandeur of the scenery, they said, would defy any attempt at describing it. What they most wondered at was the impudence of that insect, man, in daring to climb up into such regions.

My friend, the assistant magistrate, had still a fortnight of unexpired leave, and proposed to me that we should pay a visit to a friend of his at an out-of-the-way station, called Bijnore. I had not the least objection, and thither we went. We were most hospitably received, partly out of regard for ourselves in particular, but chiefly because our host had not seen a white face for five weeks.

The cutcherry, or court-house, was undergoing repair, and the magistrate, therefore, was obliged to administer the duties of his office in his own abode, or rather in the verandah; for a large number of half-clad natives in a hot country do not impart to a confined space an agreeable perfume by any means. To me this scene—the native court—was particularly interesting. There sat the covenanted official in an arm-chair, with his solah hat on and a cheroot in his mouth, listening very attentively to the sheristadar, or head clerk, who was reading or singing aloud the entire proceedings in the case then pending.

The prisoner, surrounded by half-a-dozen native policemen, all with drawn swords, was standing ten paces off. Ever and anon he interrupted the court by protesting his innocence, and assuring the Sahib that the whole of the depositions were false from beginning to end. This interruption was usually—I may say invariably—rebuked by the words, 'Choop raho, suer!' ('Hold your tongue, you pig!') And, not unfrequently the nearest policeman accompanied this mandate by giving the culprit a smart blow on the back or a 'dig in the ribs.' I have seen prisoners well thrashed in our Indian courts of justice by order of the presiding magistrate for talking out of their turn; but that was not the case in the present instance.

No more violence was resorted to than was absolutely necessary for the maintenance of order and the progress of the trial. The offence of which the prisoner stood charged was that of forging a bond for five hundred rupees, and suing thereon for principal and interest. The defence was, that the signature to the bond was not a forgery, and that the money had been advanced to the prosecutor; to prove which, no fewer than seven witnesses were called. Each of them swore, point blank, that, upon a certain day and at a certain place, they saw the prisoner pay over the money, and saw the prosecutor execute the deed. To rebuke this, the prosecutor called eleven witnesses who swore, point blank, that, upon the day and at the hour mentioned as the day and hour on which the deed was executed, they met the prosecutor at a village forty miles distant from Bijnore. In short, if their testimony was to be relied upon, the eleven witnesses had proved an alibi.

This was one of those cases which happen continually in courts of justice in India; where the magistrate or judge must not be, and is not, guided by the oaths of the witnesses, but entirely by circumstances. It is one of those cases, too, in which it would be dangerous to consult the native officers of the court; for having received bribes from both parties, their advice would be dictated entirely by pecuniary considerations. With them the question would be simply out of which party— the accused or the prosecutor—could most money be got in the event of 'guilty' or 'not guilty.' With regard to the characters of the witnesses, they are pretty equal, and generally very bad on both sides. Indeed, in nearly all these cases, the witnesses are professionals; that is to say, men who are accustomed to sell their oaths, and who thoroughly understand their business. They know exactly what to say when they come into court, just as an actor, who is letter perfect in his part, knows what to say when he comes on the boards. In fact, a case is got up exactly as a play is. Each man has his particular part and studies it separately; before the day of trial comes they meet and rehearse, and go through 'the business' till they verily believe (such is my opinion) that they are not perjured, but are speaking the truth. As for shaking the testimony of men so trained to speak to a certain string of facts, I would defy the most eminent nisi prius advocate in Europe. Besides, even if you should reject one part of a statement, it does not follow, in a native court, that you should reject the whole. The price paid to these professional witnesses depends, in a great measure, on the nature and magnitude of the cause. It is about twelve per cent out of the sum in dispute. I believe it is distributed amongst the witnesses, and the like sum amongst the native officers of the court. This, of course, does not include little extra presents given secretly to those who are supposed to have the greatest amount of influence with the Sahib, and who pretend that they will speak to him favourably. The personal servants, also, of the European magistrate or judge expect some gratuity, and hang about a client like the servants of badly regulated hotels where attendance is not charged in the bill. It is this that makes litigation so expensive in India that even the successful party is often ruined before the suit is half concluded.

'Tiffin is ready, Sahib,' said the khansamah, coming into the verandah, and placing his hands together in a supplicating attitude. 'It is on the table, Sahib.'

'Then we will adjourn,' said the magistrate, bowing to me, and rising. This was at once the signal for breaking up the day's proceedings.

The tiffin over, we began to play at whist, and continued to do so until the sun had lost his power, when the buggies were ordered, and we took a drive in couples along a very bad road. It fell to my lot to be the companion of the magistrate, a very able and excellent man: one of the most efficient officers in the East India Company's civil service. He was, moreover, an admirable linguist, and spoke Hindostanee as well as any native.

'You understood the proceedings to-day?' he asked me.

'I followed them, yes.'

'And you heard the evidence?'

'Yes.'

'What would you say? Is he guilty or not?'

'I cannot say, although I have thought a good deal on the point. Even while we were playing whist, to-day's proceedings were uppermost in my mind. Nothing can be clearer than that either one side or the other is perjured.'

'Both sides are perjured. If the bond be genuine, the men who really witnessed the execution and who subscribed their names as witnesses will not come forward, or else they are such fools that the native lawyer for the defence will not trust to them lest they should be confused and commit themselves.'

'But what do you think? Is the bond a genuine document or not?'

'That is the very question. And when there is no evidence to weigh, how are you to act?'

'I suppose that in those cases you give the prisoner the benefit of the doubt?' I remarked.

'Not always. If I did that, I should acquit almost every culprit that is brought before me, and so would every judge throughout the length and breadth of the land. By the way, about a year ago, I sent a case to the sessions judge—a case of murder. I fancied there could be no doubt as to the guilt of the accused; which was the opinion of the sessions judge and of the Sudder Court of Appeal. The man was hanged about six weeks ago; and now I have discovered, beyond all question, that he was hanged for the offence of which his prosecutor was guilty! It may be all very well for people in England to rail at the administration of justice in this country; but they would be less severe upon some of us if they could only come out here and see the material with which we have to deal. The administration of justice may be, I confess, very much reformed and improved, but where the great bulk of the people are corrupt, it can scarcely be in anything like a perfect state.' This statement, remember, was made, by a magistrate who speaks as well as writes the native language as well as the natives themselves. But conceive the confusion and injustice in those courts, where the magistrates solely depend on corrupt moonshees for what they know of the evidence.

There is but very little twilight in India; and by the time that we had returned from the drive it was dark. Shortly afterwards, dinner was announced. Dinner over, we resumed our whist, and played until midnight.

The following day was a native holiday—a Hindoo holiday. What with Hindoo holidays and Mahommedan holidays, nearly a third of every year is wasted: for, upon these days public business is suspended and the various offices closed. It is devoutly to be hoped that, when our rule in India is completely re-established, these absurd concessions—these mere pretexts for idleness—will no longer be suffered to prevail. It is only the pampered native servants of the Government, civil and military, who are clamorous for the observance of these 'great days,' as they call them. Go into the fields or ride through a bazaar on one of these holidays and you will see the people at their work, and the shopkeepers pursuing their respective avocations. You pass the court-house, the treasury, the magistrate's office, and observe that they are all shut up. You ask the reason, and are informed that it is a native holiday. You go to an establishment founded and conducted by private enterprise—a printing-office, for instance—and you observe Hindoos of every caste, and Mussulmans also, at their daily labour. Why? Because the head of such an establishment stipulates that those who wish for employ must work all the year round, and they prefer employ on such terms to no employ at all. So it is in some mercantile firms in Calcutta, and at the other Presidencies; albeit such firms experience very great inconvenience from the circumstance of the Government banks being closed on these holidays; if a merchant wishes to get a cheque cashed, or a bill discounted, he must wait sometimes for days together. Even the doors of the Queen's courts are often closed, and the judges and the counsel left unemployed, notwithstanding that the litigants are British subjects; and this because the native writers in these courts and the officers attached to them, are paid by the Company's Government, which recognises absence from duty on these holidays.

It would be hard to deprive either of the great sects of certain holidays in every year. The Doorgah-Poojah, for instance, or the Mohurrum; but it is sheer folly, and profitless withal, to sanction these constantly repeated interruptions to public business. The idlers of the covenanted civil service in India are, naturally, in favour of closing the doors of the various offices as often as possible; but the hard-working portion, those men who take some interest in the discharge of the duties for which they draw their pay, regard the native holidays as an intolerable nuisance which ought, long since, to have been abolished.

Whilst we were enjoying ourselves after dinner, on the evening of the Hindoo holiday, the khansamah came in, and announced that two Sahibs had arrived.

'Two Sahibs?' said our host. 'Who are they?'

'They are strangers to me, Sahib,' said the khansamah, 'and they do not speak Hindostanee; but their bearers say that they are Lord Sahibs.'

'Who on earth can they be?' said the magistrate of Bijnore (loudly) to himself; and, rising, he left the table to make inquiry in person, and offer the travellers every hospitality.

'O, I beg your pardon,' said a voice from one of the palanquins. 'But would you be good enough to tell me where I am?'

'You are at Bijnore,' said the magistrate, blandly.

'Bij-what?'

'Bijnore.'

'Then, how far am I from Meerut?'

'A very considerable distance—forty miles at least.'

'How the deuce is that?'

'Well, sir—in the words of the Eton Latin Grammar—I may reply:—

Felix qui potuit rerum cognoscere causas.

But where have you come from?'

'From Seharry something or other; but confound these nores, and pores, and bores! There's no recollecting the name of any place, for an hour together. The magistrate—I forget his name just now; but it was Radley, Bradley, Bagley, Ragley, or Cragley, or some such name—told me he would push me on to Meerut, and here am I, it seems, forty miles out of my road! Well, look here. I am Lord Jamleigh.'

'Indeed! Well, you are welcome to some refreshment and repose in my home, in common with your friend; and whenever you desire to be 'pushed on,' I will exert my authority to the utmost to further your views.'

'O, thank you. My friend is my valet. Here, Mexton, jump out and take my things into a room.'

While Mexton is obeying this order, and while his lordship is following his host, let us inform the reader who his lordship was, and what was the object of his mission to India.

His lordship was a young nobleman, who was about to enter Parliament, and, being desirous of acquiring information concerning India in order to be very strong when the question for renewing the charter came on in eighteen hundred and fifty-two or fifty-three, he resolved on travelling in the country for a few months: the entire period of his absence from home, including the journey overland, not to exceed half a year. After a passage of thirty-four days—having already seen the Island of Ceylon, and approved of it—his lordship landed at Madras, was carried up to Government house, where he took a hasty tiffin, and was then carried back to the beach, whence he reembarked on board the steamer, and was, three days afterwards, landed at the Ghaut in Calcutta, where he found a carriage ready to convey him to the vice-regal dwelling. After two days' stay, he was 'pushed on,' at his own request, to the Upper Provinces: his destination being Lahore. The newspapers got hold of his name, and came out with something of this kind:—'Amongst the passengers by the *Bentinck* is Lord Jamleigh, eldest son of the Right Honourable the Earl of Dapperleigh. His lordship leaves Calcutta this evening, and will pass through the following stations.' Then came a list. At many of the stations he was met—officiously met, by gentlemen in authority, who dragged—literally dragged—him, in their anxiety to have a lord for a guest, to their houses, and kept him there as long as they could: taking care to have the north-west journals informed of where and with whom his lordship had put up. He was not allowed to stay at a dâk bungalow for an hour or two, and then proceed, taking—in the strictest sense of the phrase—his bird's-eye view of India, its people, its institutions, and so forth. Some of them threw obstacles in the way of his getting bearers, so that he might remain with them for four-and-twenty hours, and thus thoroughly impregnate and air their houses with an aristocratical atmosphere. Others lugged him to their courts and collectorates, albeit he had seen one of each at Burdwan and Bengal, and consequently had seen the working of the Indian judicial and revenue departments, and knew all about them! This sycophantic importunity of a few government officials soured his lordship's temper, which imparted to his manners a rudeness which was perhaps foreign to his nature. His lordship was led to believe that *all* Indian officials were a parcel of sycophants—progress-impeding sycophants—and hence he grew to treat them all alike: and he did not scruple, at last, to extract his information from them much in the same way that a petulant judge who has lost all patience with a rambling witness, takes him out of the hands of counsel, and brings him sharply to the point. For instance, 'I know all about that, but tell me this,'—note-book in hand—would Lord Jamleigh in such wise frequently interrogate his civil hosts, who insisted on doing themselves the honour of entertaining his lordship. The fact was that, in his own opinion, he knew all about India and its affairs long before he touched the soil, for he had read a good deal in blue books and newspapers. His object, as we have before hinted, was simply to see the country and travel in it, or through it, and thus arm himself with a tremendous and telling weapon in a contested debate, should he take part therein. And therefore when his lordship asked questions it was not so much with a view to obtain information as to test the accuracy of that already acquired by reading, over the fireside in the library, of his father's mansion in Bagdad Square. Thus, the entries in his lordship's note-book were, after all, merely a matter of form.

Having divested himself of the dust with which he was

covered, and having restored himself to his personal comforts, his lordship joined our little party, and partook of some dinner which the khansamah had prepared for him. His repast concluded, his lordship moistened his throat with a glass of cool claret, and proceeded, in his own manner, to interrogate his host, who was not only an accomplished scholar, but a ready and refined wit. It was thus that the dialogue was commenced and continued:—

'What is the number of inhabitants in this district?' asked the noble guest.

'Upon my word I don't know; I have never counted them,' said the host.

'But have you no idea? Can't you give a guess?'

'Oh, yes; some hundreds of thousands.'

'Ah! And crime—much crime!' his lordship persevered.

'Very much. But we are going to reduce it, during the ensuing half-year, exactly thirty-three and a-half per cent,' answered the magistrate, looking uncommonly statistical.

'How?'

'Well, that is what my assistant and myself have decided upon.'

'I do not understand you. How can you possibly say at this moment whether, during the next six months, the amount of crime shall be greater or less?' His lordship was puzzled.

'How? Why just in the same way that the directors of a joint-stock bank determine in their parlour what shall be the amount of dividend payable to shareholders. My assistant wanted to make a reduction of fifty per centum on the last returns; but I think thirty-three and a-half will be a very fair figure.'

'You intend, perhaps, to be more severe?' said the young legislator.

'Nothing of the kind. On the contrary, we intend to be less energetic by thirty-three and a-half per cent—to take matters more easily, in short.'

'I wish I knew what you meant.'

'I will explain it to you.'

'As briefly as possible, please.' His lordship did not want to be bored, evidently.

'By all means.'

'I only want facts, you see.'

'And I am about to give you facts—dry facts.'

'Well?'

'The facts are these. There is a district in these provinces nearly twice the size of this, and it contains nearly double the number of inhabitants.'

'Yes.'

'During the past half-year, the number of convictions in that district has been very much less than the number of convictions in this district. And the Sudder Court of Appeal has come to the conclusion, on looking at the figures in the official return, that the proportion of crime to population, in this district, is greater than it is in that district.'

'Very naturally.'

'Indeed? But suppose that the magistrate of that district only attends his court once or twice a-week, and then only for an hour or two on those days; and suppose that his assistant is a young man who makes sport his occupation and his business, and his recreation and his sport. And suppose that I and my assistant work hard, and do our best to hunt up all the murderers, thieves, and other culprits, whom we hear of, and bring them to justice and to punishment. What then? Are the figures in the official returns, touching the convictions, to be taken as any criterion of the crime perpetrated in our respective districts?' His worship delivered these questions triumphantly.

'In that case, certainly not.'

'Well, the Sudder have looked at the convictions, and the consequence has been, that in the last printed report issued by that august body (composed of three old and imbecile gentlemen) to the Government, the magistrate of that district and his assistant have been praised for their zeal, and recommended for promotion, while the magistrate and assistant of this district have been publicly censured; or, to use the cant phrase of the report, 'handed up for the consideration of the Most Noble the Governor-General of India.'

'Is it possible?' asked the Lord, throwing up his hands.

'You ask for dry facts, and I have given you dry facts.'

'May I make a note of this?' (pulling out an elegant souvenir). 'Not that I should think of mentioning your name.'

'You may make a note of it; and, so far as mentioning my name is concerned, you may do as you please. I have already written to the Sudder what I have stated to you,' was the answer.

'What! about the thirty-three and a-half per cent?'

'Yes, and, what is more, I have insisted on a copy of the letter being forwarded to the Governor-General.'

'And what will be the result, do you suppose?'

'I neither know nor care. I have just served my time in this penal country; and, being entitled to both my pardon and my pension, I intend to apply shortly for both.'

The reader will be glad to hear that a long correspondence ensued on this subject between the Sudder, the Government, and the mutinous magistrate. The upshot was, that the imbecile old men who had too long warmed that tribunal were pushed off their stools by the Governor-General (Lord Dalhousie), who, very meritoriously, bullied them into resigning the service; threatening, as some say, to hold a commission on their capacity for office. In their stead were appointed three gentlemen, whose abilities and vigour had hitherto been kept in the back settlements of India. The crowning point of all was, that the mutinous magistrate was one of the illustrious three!

Lord Jamleigh informed us that he had seen Lahore, and that he was about to go across the country to Bombay, and that he should then have seen all three Presidencies, as well as all the Upper Provinces, and the Punjab. He regretted, half apologetically, that he had not been able to take a look at the Himalayas, Simlah and Mussoorie; but the fact was, 'he was so much pressed for time.'

'Poor devils!' exclaimed our host, smiling. 'But, as they won't know anything about it, they won't feel it much—indeed, not at all.'

'To whom are you alluding?' asked my lord.

'The Himalayas,' sighed our host, passing the claret to his lordship, who, by this time, had discovered that he had not got into a nest of sycophants, who worshipped a title, no matter how frivolous or how insolent the man might be who wore it; but that he had accidentally fallen into the company of persons of independent character; and albeit, they were desirous of giving him a welcome and making him comfortable—being a stranger who had lost his way— nevertheless, were determined to make him pay in some shape for the want of courtesy he had exhibited when the bearers set his *palkee* down at the door of the bungalow. This discovery made his lordship a little uncomfortable, and rather cautious in his observations. He felt, in short, as one who knows that he has committed an error, and that some penalty will be exacted; but what penalty, and how exacted, he cannot imagine. Had he been able to get away, he would probably have taken a hasty farewell of us. But that was impossible. His jaded bearers were cooking their food, and, until twelve o'clock, there was no hope of getting them together.

The khansamah came in with a fresh bottle of wine. Our host, withdrawing his cigar from his lips, inquired of him if the wants of the gentleman's servant had been attended to.

'Yes, Sahib,' was the reply.

'And have you given him any champagne?'

'No, Sahib.'

'Then do.'

'Oh, pray do nothing of the kind!' exclaimed his Lordship. 'He is not accustomed to it.'

'Then he will enjoy it all the more,' said our host. 'I hope he is taking notes, and will write a book on India. I should much like to see his impressions in print; and he may possibly dignify me by devoting a few lines to the character of my hospitality. It is to be hoped, however, that, should his travel inspire him with a thirst for literary distinction, he will confine himself to a personal compilation of his experience, and not go into judicial or revenue matters; for, should he do so, you may find yourself clashing with him, and that would be awkward. His publisher's critic might be inclined to break a spear with your publisher's critic, in their respective reviews of your respective works, and it would be quite impossible to conjecture where the controversy might end. Indisposed as I am, generally, to obtrude my advice upon any one, and much less on a perfect stranger, I nevertheless feel that I am only doing you a kindness when I say that, if I were you, I would regard Hindostan as a sort of Juan Fernandez, myself the Crusoe thereof, and this valet as my man Friday; and then, with a due observance of that line of demarcation which should always be drawn between civilised man and the savage, I would not permit him to keep even a stick whereon to notch the day or time of any particular event that occurred during my residence in the country, lest he should some day or other—in consequence of my having discharged him, or he having discharged me—rise up and instigate some man or other to call in question the accuracy of my facts. The wine is with you; will you fill, and pass it on?'

Lord Jamleigh became very red in the face, and rather confused both in manner and speech. As for myself and the two assistant magistrates, there was something so benignant in the expression of our host's handsome and dignified countenance—something so quaintly sarcastic in the tone and manner of his discourse, that, had we known that death was the penalty of not maintaining the gravity of our features, our lives would certainly have been forfeited.

A silence for several minutes ensued; and then Lord Jamleigh spoke to our host as follows:—

'Most of the young noblemen who come to this country, come only to travel about and amuse themselves. I come on business—I may say, Parliamentary business. My time is short, and I must make the most of it. I dare say, when you saw my name in the papers, as having arrived in India, you little thought that I was not a man of pleasure and excursion?'

'Upon my word, the subject never once became a matter of speculation with me,' said our host.

After some further conversation, in which our host spared his visitor as little as was consistent with good breeding, Lord Jamleigh, who had been 'sitting upon thorns,' rose and said:—

'I am afraid I have already trespassed on your goodness too long. I will not attempt to apolo—apolo—or to express how much—how much; nor to assure you that—assure you—that when—'

'Oh, pray don't mention it!' said our host, smiling. 'You desire your *palkee*?'

'If you please,' said Lord Jamleigh.

The palkee was ordered, and we were standing in expectation that it would be instantly announced as 'ready,' when the sirdar-bearer (head personal attendant) came into the room, in a state of excessive trepidation, and informed us that the Sahib's Sahib (Lord Jamleigh's valet) was drunk, asleep, and refused to be disturbed on any pretence whatever.

This announcement, which caused general merriment, induced Lord Jamleigh to ejaculate:—

'That's the champagne, I suspected as much!'

'Where is he?' inquired our host of the sirdar-bearer. 'In his palkee?'

'No, Sahib,' was the reply. 'He is lying on that Sahib's bed,' pointing to me.

Here, again, everybody laughed, except myself. I was rather angry, being somewhat particular on this point. So I suggested that he might be put into his vehicle at once. The native servants, of course, were afraid to touch him, lest he should awake and 'hit out;' so we, the five of us, Europeans, the magistrate, the two assistant magistrates, Lord Jamleigh, and myself, had to lift, remove, and pack in his palkee, the overcome, and perfectly unconscious valet. He must have been sipping brandy-and-water before he came to the bungalow, for he had only half finished his bottle of champagne. Lord Jamleigh now got into his palanquin, and composed himself for the night, or, rather, the remainder of it, and in order that there might be no mistake as to his Lordship's destination, the magistrate sent a horseman to accompany the cortège, with directions that 'the Sahibs' were to be taken to Durowlah, on the road to Meerut, and to the house of the magistrate, by whom Lord Jamleigh had been invited, or rather, 'petitioned,' to stay with him, should he pass through that station, and (to use his Lordship's own terms), as he had promised to do so, he supposed that he must keep his word. When a palanquin is escorted by a sowar, the sowar when the destination is approached, rides on and gives notice that a lady, or gentleman, as the case may be, is coming; and, as the natives of India can never pronounce European names properly, the precaution is usually taken of writing down the name of the traveller on a card, or a slip of paper, and giving it to the sowar. In this case, 'Viscount Jamleigh' was written down for the guidance and information of the Durowlah functionary.

It was about seven a.m. when this card was put into the hands of the gentleman who had invited Lord Jamleigh; whom, by the way, he had never seen. The bungalow was immediately all life and in commotion; the servants ordered to prepare tea and coffee; the best bed-room vacated by the present occupants; hot water in readiness; and ere long a *palkee*—a single *palkee*—loomed in the distance; the other *palkee* was a long way, some three miles, behind. One of the bearers who was carrying it, had fallen and injured himself, and thus was a delay of an hour and a-half occasioned. And during that hour and-half a pretty mistake was committed. The first *palkee* was that containing the valet, and the one behind was that of his lordship. The valet had not recovered the effects of his potations; and, on being awakened, seemed, and really was, bewildered and stupified—so much so, that he could not inform the magistrate that he was 'only a servant,' and not entitled to the attentions that were showered upon him. With trembling hand, he took the cup of tea from the silver salver, and gazing wildly round, murmured, rather than said—

'Brandy! Little Brandy!' which was at once brought and administered. He then had his warm 'wash,' sat down on the best bed, and suffered himself to be punkahed by two domestics in snow-white garments. This revived him somewhat; but still he felt far too ill to talk. He simply shook his head, and there was a good deal of meaning in that shake, if the magistrate could only have understood it.

'Take some brandy and soda-water, my lord,' said his host.

The valet nodded assent.

The magistrate mixed the dose, and administered it with his own hands.

The valet sighed, and again shook his head.

'You will be better presently, my lord,' said the magistrate.

'Drunk as a lord!' hiccuped the valet.

'O, no, my lord! It was the jolting along the road.'

'In that coffin?' said the valet, who now began to regain the use of his tongue.

'Yes, my lord.'

'Am I a lord? He, he, he! Where am I?'

'At Durowlah, my lord.'

'And who are *you?*'

'Your host, my lord.'

'Then this is not the station-house?'

'Not exactly, my lord.'

'Give us a little drop more of that last brew.'

'Yes, my lord.'

'Ah! Thank you! I feel better now—much better. It was that champagne. Good it was, though. What place was that we were at?'

'Bijnore, my lord.'

'I'm not a lord.'

'Would that I were in your place, my lord!'

'Well, it isn't a bad place,' grinned the valet. 'Plenty to eat and drink, little to do, and good wages. But hang this Hindyer! It was a mistake altogether!'

The magistrate took this for fun, laughed immensely, and then said:—

'We had Lord Frederick Pontasguieure staying with us for a week, last winter. A very amusing character he was.'

'O, had you? Was he amusing? O! We don't keep his company. Don't know him. I'd give a five-pound note to be in Piccadilly at this moment. This is a nice mess. But the traps are all right, I see. There's the dressing-case, and the writing-desk, and the little medicine-chest.'

'Recline upon the bed, my lord, and have a gentle sleep. The punkah, you will find, will very speedily lull you to repose.'

'Well, I will,' said the valet; and soon fell fast asleep. The venetians were then closed, and the house kept as quiet as possible.

When Lord Jamleigh himself arrived, and established his identity, the scene that ensued may be easily imagined.

The magistrate, with a marvellous want of tact, acknowledged the mistake that he had made: told, in fact, the whole uncomplimentary truth. Lord Jamleigh, and perhaps with reason, was dreadfully annoyed at the idea that the servant should have been mistaken for himself; but he let out, however, that was the third time the thing had happened, and that in future he should insist upon the fellow wearing livery, instead of plain clothes, and a black wide-awake hat.

The valet was speedily lifted out of the best bed, and transferred to another apartment, where he slept himself sober, and arose at about half-past one to explain to his lordship that he was not much in fault.

I would advise all noblemen and gentlemen who, like Lord Jamleigh, would take a bird's-eye look at India, not to travel with an European servant, who, in that country, is as helpless as an infant, and quite as troublesome, besides being in the way of everybody in every house. It is, moreover, cruel to the servant. He can talk to no one, and becomes perfectly miserable.

Miscellaneous

THE HOUSE OF a civilian (a magistrate and collector) in the heart of a district, such as Bijnore, is really worthy of contemplation. With the exception of a bungalow, which is usually occupied by the assistant, and which may, therefore, be said to belong to the magistrate's house, there is no other Christian abode within five-and-thirty or forty miles. The house is usually well, but not extravagantly, furnished; the walls are adorned with prints and pictures, and the shelves well stored with books. In a word, if the punkahs and the venetian blinds, the therm-antidotes, and sundry other Indian peculiarities were removed, you might fancy yourself in some large country-house in England.

There was at Bijnore a native moonshee who was a very good scholar; and, as I was anxious to read Hindostanee and Persian with him (the more especially as I much enjoyed the society of mine host and his assistant), I was induced to accept an invitation to remain for a month. During this period I studied for several hours a day, besides attending the Court House regularly, to listen to the proceedings, and acquire some knowledge of a most extraordinary jargon, composed of a little Hindostanee, a little Persian, and a good deal of Arabic. This jargon is known in India as the language of the courts. A good Persian and Hindostanee scholar cannot understand it, unless he is accustomed to it. Many magistrates and judges have insisted upon having pure Hindostanee spoken; but to no purpose. Up to a recent period, Persian mixed with Arabic was the language in which legal proceedings were conducted—Persian and Arabic being as foreign languages to the people of India as English, German, or French. And, when the order went forth that Hindostanee was to be used, the native officers of the courts, and the native lawyers who practised therein, complied with it by putting a Hindostanee verb at the end of each sentence, and using the Hindostanee pronouns, retaining in all their integrity (or rascality) the Persian and Arabic adverbs, prepositions, nouns, adjectives, and conjunctions. An indigo planter in Tahoot, who spoke Hindostanee perfectly, having lived amongst the natives for upwards of twenty years, assured me that he did not comprehend a single sentence of a decree in court Hindostanee, that he heard read out to him—a decree in a case to which he was a party. What is even more absurd, each court has its own peculiar jargon, so that the magistrate or judge, who from long experience has acquired a thorough knowledge of the jargon of his own court, has very great difficulty in comprehending the jargon of another court. This might be altered by fining any officer of court, or native lawyer, who, in matters connected with a suit, used words and phrases unintelligible to the mass of the people; but the order would have to emanate from Government. No magistrate or judge would venture on even an attempt to bring about so desirable a reform.

Whilst at Bijnore, I was seized with an attack of tic-douloureux, and suffered all its extreme agonies. One of my host's servants informed me that there was a very clever native doctor in the village, who could immediately assuage any pain—tooth-ache, for instance—and he begged permission to bring him to see me. I consented.

The native doctor was a tall, thin Mussulman, with a lofty forehead, small black eyes, long aquiline nose, and finely chiselled mouth and chin. His hair, eye-brows, and long beard were of a yellowish white, or cream colour. Standing before me in his skull-cap, he was about the most singular looking person I ever beheld. His age did not exceed forty-four or forty-five years. He put several questions to me, but I was in too great pain to give him any replies. He begged of me to sit down. I obeyed him, mechanically. Seating himself in a chair immediately opposite to me, he looked very intently into my eyes. After a little while, his gaze became disagreeable, and I endeavoured to turn my head aside, but I was unable to do so. I now felt that I was being mesmerized. Observing, I suppose, an expression of anxiety, if not of fear, on my features, he bade me not to be alarmed. I longed to order him to cease; but, as the pain was becoming less and less acute, and as I retained my consciousness intact, I suffered him to proceed. To tell the truth, I doubt whether I could have uttered a sound. At all events, I did not make the attempt. Presently, that is to say, after two or three minutes, the pain had entirely left me, and I felt what is commonly called, all in a glow. The native doctor now removed his eyes from off mine, and inquired if I were better. My reply, which I had no difficulty in giving at once, was in the affirmative; in short, that I was completely cured. Observing that he placed his hands over his head, and pressed his skull, I asked him if he were suffering.

'Yes, slightly,' was his reply; 'but I am so accustomed to it, it gives me but little inconvenience.'

I then begged of him to explain to me how it was that he had the power to afford me such miraculous relief. That, he said, he was unable to do. He did not know. I then talked to him of mesmerism and of the wonderful performances of Dr. Esdaile, in the Calcutta hospital. He had lately heard of mesmerism, he said; but, years before he heard of it, he was in the habit of curing people by assuaging their pain. The gift had been given to him soon after he attained manhood. That, with one exception, and that was in the case of a Keranee—a half-caste—no patient had ever fallen asleep, or had become *beehosh* (unconscious), under his gaze. 'The case of the half-caste,' he went on to say, 'alarmed me. He fell asleep, and slept for twelve hours, snoring like a man in a state of intoxication.' I was not the first European he had operated upon, he said; that in Bareilly, where he formerly lived, he had afforded relief to many officers and to several ladies. Some had tooth-ache, some tic-douloureux, some other pains. 'But,' he exclaimed, energetically, 'the most extraordinary case I ever had, was that of a Sahib who had gone mad— 'drink delirious.' His wife would not suffer him to be strapped down, and he was so violent that it took four or five other Sahibs to hold him. I was sent for, and, at first, had great difficulty with him and much trembling. At last, however, I locked his eyes up, as soon as I got him to look at me, and kept him for several hours as quiet as a mouse, during which time he had no brandy, no wine, no beer; and, though he did not sleep, he had a good long rest. I stayed with him for two days, and whatever I told him to do he did immediately. He had great sorrow on his mind, poor man. Three of his children had died of fever within one short week, and he had lost much money by the failure of an agency-house in Calcutta. There was a cattle serjeant, too, an European, whom I also cured of that drinking madness by locking up his eyes.'

'What do you mean by locking up his eyes?'

'Well, what I did with you; I locked up your eyes. When I got his eyes fixed on mine, he could not take them away— could not move.'

'But can you lock up any one's eyes in the way that you locked up mine?'

'No, not everybody's. There was an artillery captain once who defied me to lock up his eyes. I tried very hard; but, instead of locking up his, he locked up mine, and I could not move till he permitted me. And there was a lady, the wife of a judge, who had pains in the head, which I could not cure, because she locked up my eyes. With her I trembled much, by straining every nerve, but it was of no use.'

'Do you know any other native who has the same power that you possess?'

'Only three; but, I dare say, there may be hundreds in these provinces who have it, and who use it. And now, Sahib,' said the native doctor, taking from his kummerbund (the cloth that encircles the waist) a bundle of papers, 'I desire to show you some of my certificates, at the same time to beg of you to pardon my apparent want of respect in appearing in your presence in this skull-cap instead of a turban; but the fact is, that when I heard you were in such great pain, I did not think it humane to delay until I had adorned myself.'

I proceeded to examine very carefully every one of his many certificates; not that I was in any way interested in them, but because I knew it would afford him great pleasure. In all, they were quite as numerous as those which English charlatans publish in testimony of their skill in extracting corns. They were more elaborate however; for it is by the length of a certificate that a native judges of its value—just in the same way that Partridge, when Tom Jones took him to see *Hamlet*, admired the character of the King, because he spoke louder than any of the company, 'anybody could see that he was a king.' As for myself, I sat down and covered a whole sheet of foolscap in acknowledgment of my gratitude to Mustapha Khan Bahadoor, for having delivered me from unendurable torments. To my certificate I pinned a cheque on the North-West Bank for one hundred rupees (ten pounds), and, presenting both documents to the doctor, permitted him to take his leave. Some months afterwards, on discovering that this cheque had not been presented for payment, I wrote to the assistant magistrate, and asked him, as a favour, to send for the native doctor, and obtain some information on the subject. In reply, I was informed that the doctor preferred keeping the cheque appended to my certificate as an imperishable memorial of the extraordinary value in which his services had been held by an European gentleman, and that he would not part with it for ten times the amount in gold or silver. Such a strange people are the natives of India! Their cupidity is enormous certainly, but their vanity (I am speaking of the better class) is even greater. One hundred rupees was equal to half a year's earnings of the native doctor, and yet he preferred holding the useless autograph of an insignificant Sahib like myself for the amount rather than realize it. The native doctor evidently reasoned thus:—'I might spend the one hundred rupees, might not be believed if I made the assertion that I had received it; but here is the voucher.' Some may imagine that he kept it as a sort of decoy-duck; but this I am perfectly satisfied was not the case.

I was now about to leave Bijnore, and, as time was of no object to me, I made up my mind to travel no more by palkee, or horse dâk, but in the most independent and comfortable manner. I therefore provided myself with two small tents, and two camels to carry them, two bullocks to carry the tent furniture, my baggage, and stores; a pony for my own riding, and a similar animal for a boy khitmutghur, who was also my personal servant or bearer.

I engaged also a cook and a sweeper, or general helper; so that, when the sawans (camel drivers), the bullock-man, and the syces (grooms), were included, my establishment numbered, in all, eight servants, whose pay in the aggregate amounted to fifty rupees (five pounds) per mensem. This, of course, included their 'keep,' for they provided themselves with food. The expense of keeping the camels, the bullocks, and the ponies, was, in all, thirty-five rupees (three pounds fifteen shillings) per mensem; while my own expenses, including everything (except beer and cheroots), were not in excess of fifty rupees per month; so that I was thus enabled to travel about India at a cost of not more than two hundred pounds per annum, or two hundred and twenty-five pounds at the very outside. The reader must remember that in almost every one of the villages in India, fowls, eggs, rice, flour, native vegetables, curry stuff, and milk are procurable, and at very small prices, if your servants do not cheat you, and mine did not; for I made an agreement with my boy khitmutghur to that effect; indeed, I entered into a regular contract with him previous to starting, touching the purchase of every article that would be required during my journey. This boy was, in short, my commissariat department. His name was Shumsheer (a word signifying in the Persian language, 'a sword'), but he generally went by the name of Sham. He had been for several months in the service of the assistant magistrate of Bijnore; who, as a very great favour, permitted the boy to accompany me on my travels; he was so clever, so sharp, so intelligent, and so active a servant. He was not more than sixteen, and very short, for his age; but stoutly built, and as strong as a young lion. He was, moreover, very good-looking, and had, for a native of Hindoostan, a very fair complexion. He had been for several years the servant, or page, of an officer on the staff of a Governor-General, and he spoke English with considerable fluency, but with an idiom so quaint, that it was amusing in the last degree to listen to him. He had been 'spoilt,' in one sense of the word, while at Government House, not only by his own master, but by the whole staff, who had encouraged him to give his opinions on all subjects with a freedom which was at first very disagreeable to me. But, ere long, I too encouraged him to do so; his opinions were so replete with such strong common sense, and were expressed in such an original fashion. If an inquiry touching a certain administration had been called for by Parliament, what an invaluable witness would that boy have been before a Committee of either house—provided he had not been previously 'tampered with.'

When all my preparations had been completed, I took leave of my friends, and left Bijnore at three o'clock one morning. My destination was Umballah. I did not take the main road; but a shorter cut across the country, conducted by a guide who knew the district well, and who was enjoined to procure for me another guide as soon as his information failed him.

By seven o'clock we had travelled over twelve miles of ground, and as the sun was beginning to be very warm, I commanded a halt. Our tents were then pitched beneath a tope (cluster) of mango-trees whose branches formed a dense shade. Having bathed, breakfasted, smoked, and read several pages of a Persian book, I fell asleep, and was not awakened until noon, when Sham came into my tent and reported that there was an abundance of black partridge in the neighbourhood: he then proposed that I should dine early—at one p.m.—and at half past four take my gun; and, permitting him to take another, sally forth in search of the game. To this proposal I at once assented, and removing my camp stool to the opening of my little hill tent, I looked out into the fields, where I saw some men ploughing. For the first time during my travels I was struck with the appearance of the instrument which the natives use for tilling the soil; an instrument which, in fact, closely resembles that used by the Romans, according to the directions laid down in the Georgics:

'Curvi formam adcipit ulmus aratri,' &c., &c., and at first I felt some surprise that an implement so apparently ill-fitted for the purpose for which it is designed, should answer all the requirements of the cultivator. The substitution of the English plough for this native hùr has been several times projected by gentlemen who were zealous in the cause of agriculture; but without any success, or reasonable hope thereof; for when we consider the cheapness, and the great amount of labour always available, the general lightness of the soil, the inaptitude of the natives of India for great or continued physical exertion, the inferiority of the cattle, all of which are the marked characteristics of India, it would not only be undesirable, but impossible to introduce the English plough generally as an implement of husbandry—an implement requiring physical strength, manual dexterity, and a superior breed of cattle for draught. Rude and simple as the native hùr is, or as it may seem to the casual observer, cursorily viewing the operation of ploughing, it has still many good qualities which render it peculiarly suited to the genius of the Indian cultivator; and it is not in any immediate endeavour to improve it or alter it that any real benefit can be conferred on the cause of Indian agriculture. All the efforts, therefore, that have been made in that direction have been time and trouble expended to no purpose. It has been said that all improvement to be real must be spontaneous, or take rise within itself; and it would seem to be more reasonable to improve such means and appliances as the natives use and understand, without running counter to the ideas and shocking the prejudices which they entertain, by endeavouring to compel their adoption of European modes of culture, which, however well suited to the land of their origin, have not the quality most necessary to their practicability, that of being comprehensible to the people of India. The true end of agriculture:

'with artful toil

To 'meliorate and tame the stubborn soil,

To give dissimilar yet fruitful lands

The grain, or herb, or plant, that each demands,'

is best to be attained by aiding and assisting the development of those resources of the soil which have already been made visible by the people themselves.

Here it is that the duty of the Government begins. The precariousness of the land tenure is one of the greatest impediments to the outlay of capital by the tenant in the improvement of the land; and as there is but little prospect of the removal of this objection, the Government should fulfil what would, were the case different, be the obvious plans of the landholder in developing the resources of the soil. Irrigation and manure are the two great points most deserving of attention. On both points the resources of the country are incalculable; the advantages evident and immediate; both require system and an outlay of capital, which the zemindar (native landholder) is often unable, and oftener unwilling, to adopt and incur—from want of confidence in the administration of the law and the law itself. With the ryot, or cultivator, the case is very different. The law, or the administration thereof, affects him in a very slight degree compared with the zemindar. The land tenure matters very little to him; his rights have been secured; he profits by the outlay of capital on the land. Risk he has none. His advantage is immediate. But he does not possess the means of improvement in any way. He may build a well, dig a tank, or plant a grove to the memory of a departed ancestor, and by so doing enhance the value of the land to the zemindar; but he almost always ruins himself by the act, leaving his debts to be paid by his descendants, and the well, tank, or grove mortgaged to the banker for the extra expenses incurred in its establishment! It behoves an enlightened Government to do for the people and the country what they are unable to do for themselves. An inquiry properly set on foot, and undertaken by competent persons on the part of the Government, to investigate all particulars regarding the state of agriculture, would bring to light many facts, which, if made fitting use of, would not only greatly redound to the honour but adduce greatly to the advantage and profit of the State. The information thus acquired, and not founded on the reports of native (Government) collectors, police officers, and peaons (messengers), but ascertained by the personal inspection of European officials, and from the opinions of the zemindars and cultivators themselves, would enable the Government to know and devise remedies to obviate the evils arising out of the gradual decline of the agricultural classes in our earliest occupied territories. It would show the Government many places where the expenditure of four or five thousand rupees (four or five hundred pounds) in the repairs or erection of a dam, for the obstruction of some rain-filled nullah (a wide and deep ditch), would yield a return yearly of equal amount, besides affording employment, and the means of livelihood to hundreds of persons. It would show where the opening of a road, or the building of a bridge, involving but a small expenditure, would give a new life to a part of the country hitherto forgotten, and render the inhabitants flourishing and happy, by throwing open to them a market for their produce—a market at present out of their reach. It would prove incontestably that the means of irrigation—the true water-power of India, has been even more neglected than the water-power of that (in comparison with the United States) sluggish colony, Canada. The initial step once taken—the march of improvement once fairly set on foot—private enterprise, duly encouraged, will follow in the wake of the Government; and capital once invested, land in India will become intrinsically valuable, and thus obtain the attention it merits. Agricultural improvement would induce lasting and increasing prosperity of the cultivating classes (the bulk of the population) and of the country itself.

'What! Sham! Dinner ready?' I exclaimed, on observing the boy approaching the tent with a tray and a table-cloth.

'Oh, yes, sir; quite ready. And very good dinner.'

'What have you got?'

'Stewed duck, sir—curry, sir; pancake, sir. And by the time you eat that, one little quail ready, sir, with toast. I give dinner fit for a Governor-General, sir; and the silver shining like the moon, sir.'

(It was in this way that he ran on whilst laying the table.)

'But why are you preparing covers for two, when I am dining alone?'

'Yes, sir. But only poor mans has table laid for one. That place opposite is for company sake. And suppose some gentleman come—not likely here, but suppose? Then all is ready. No running about—no calling out, 'Bring plate, knife and fork, and spoon, and glass,' and all that. And if two plates laid, master, if he like—when I am standing behind his chair keeping the flies off while he eats—may fancy that some friend or some lady sitting opposite, and in his own mind he may hold some guftoogoo (conversation). That's why I lay the table for two, sir.'

I had been warned by the gentleman who permitted Sham to accompany me, that he was such an invaluable servant, it was only politic to let him have his own way in trifling matters; and therefore instead of objecting to his proceeding, I applauded his foresight.

Whilst discussing the stewed duck, which was excellent— as was indeed every dish prepared by Sham, when he had 'his own way—' and while he was standing behind me, keeping the flies off with a chowrie (a quantity of long horsehair fastened to a handle), I talked to him without turning my head:

'You say you wish to take a gun. Have you ever been out shooting?'

'Oh, yes, sir. When my master went up from Calcutta to Mussoorie and Simlah with the Governor-General, I went with him. And I often went out shooting in the Dhoon, with my master, who was a great sportsman, sir. And I was out with my master—on the same elephant—when the Governor-General shot the tiger.'

'What! Did the Governor-General shoot a tiger?'

'Oh, no, sir. But my master and the other gentlemens make him think he did, sir.'

'Explain yourself.'

'Well, sir, the Governor-General said he had heard a great deal of tiger shooting, and should like to see some for once. So my master, who was a very funny gentleman, went to an officer in the Dhoon—another very funny gentleman—and between them it was agreed that his lordship should shoot one tiger. And so they sent out some native shikarees (huntsmen), told them to wound but not kill one big tiger in the jungle, and leave him there. And the native shikarees did shoot one big tiger in the jungle, and they came and made a report where he was lying. Then next morning when all the elephants and gentlemens was ready, and the Governor-General had his gun in his hand, they all went to the jungle; and when they got to the place and heard the tiger growl very angrily, my master called out, 'There, my lord—there he is; take your shot!' and my lord fired his gun, and my master cried out very loud: 'My lord, you've hit him!' And my lord, who was very much confused—not being a sportsman—said, 'Have I?' And all the gentlemens cried out: 'Yes, my lord!' And then some of the gentlemens closed round the tiger and killed him, by firing many bullets at him. And my lord had the tiger's skin taken off, and it was sent to England to be make a carpet for my lord's sitting-room. And for many days all the gentlemens laughed, and asked of one another, 'Who shot the tiger?' And the Governor-General was so happy and so proud, and wore his head as high as a seesu-tree. But he had enough of tiger-shooting in that one tiger; for he was not a sportsman, and did not like the jolting of the elephant in the jungle.'

My repast ended, and the table-cloth removed, I lighted a cigar, and took my camp-stool once more to the opening of the tent, when, to my surprise, and somewhat to my dismay, I found myself besieged by a host of ryots, cultivators of the soil, each bearing a present in the shape of a basket of fruit or vegetables, or a brass dish covered with almonds, raisins, and native sweetmeats. These poor creatures, who doubtless fancied that I was a Sahib in authority (possibly, Sham had told them that I was a commissioner—a very great man—on a tour of inspection), prostrated themselves at my feet, and in the most abject manner imaginable craved my favour and protection. I promised each and every one of them, with much sincerity, that if ever it lay in my power to do them a service, they might depend upon my exerting myself to the utmost; and then I made a variety of inquiries touching their respective ages, families, circumstances, and prospects, in order to prove that I had already taken an interest in them. I then asked them some questions touching the game in the locality, and was glad to hear the report made by Sham confirmed to the letter. I was assured that the light jungle in the rear of my tents literally swarmed with black partridges.

It was now nearly time to go out, and in the course of two hours I brought down no less than seven brace, while Sham distinguished himself by killing five birds. By the time I returned to my tent I was weary, and retired to rest, having previously given orders that I was to be called at two a.m., insomuch as at that hour I intended to resume the march. It is one thing, however, to retire to rest, but it is another thing to sleep. What with the croaking of the frogs in a neighbouring tank, and the buzzing and biting of the musquitoes in my tent, I could not close an eye. I lay awake the whole night, thinking—thinking of a thousand things, but of home chiefly; and right glad was I when Sham approached my bed, holding in one hand a cup of very hot and strong coffee, and in the other my cigar-case, while the noise outside, incident on the striking of the tents and the breaking up of the little camp, was as the sweetest music to my ears.

Forward

I WAS TWELVE days marching from Bijnore to Umballah, and, by keeping away from the high-road, I did not see during my journey a single European face. I moved entirely amongst the people, or rather the peasantry, of the Upper Provinces of India—a very poor and very ignorant peasantry, but, comparatively speaking, civil and honest. Sham made a much greater impression upon them than I did; mounted on his pony, and dressed in very gay attire—a purple velvet tunic, pyjamahs of red silk trimmed with gold lace, a turban of very gorgeous aspect, and shoes embroidered all over with silver. He had more the appearance of a young rajah or prince than a gentleman's servant. And Sham talked to his countrymen—if the wretched Hindoos could be so called—in a lofty strain which vastly amused me, though I did not approve of it. I said nothing, however. As for the camp arrangements, he had completely taken them out of my hands, and he was so much better manager than myself that I was well content that it should be so; all that was left to me was to name the hour for departing from an encampment-ground, and the next spot whereon I wished my tents pitched.

It was past six o'clock on the morning of the 20th of

April, when I came within a few miles of Umballah. The mornings and the nights were still cool; but, in the day the heat was beginning to be very severe. However, after taking my coffee and making my toilet, I caused my pony to be re-saddled, and, followed by Sham mounted on his pony, rode into the cantonments, inquiring my way, as I went along, of the various servants who were moving about. I eventually found myself at the door of a bungalow, which was tenanted by a very old friend and distant connexion of mine. He was an officer in one of her Majesty's Regiments of Foot, then stationed at Umballah.

'You will sleep here, of course, during your stay,' he said; 'but you are the guest of the mess, remember. We have settled all that, and we will go up in the buggy presently to deposit your pasteboard in the mess reading room. I will point out to you where you will always find your knife and fork, and I will introduce to you all the servants—the mess-sergeant especially.'

I must now digress for a brief while, in order to give the uninitiated reader some idea of Indian etiquette as it exists amongst Europeans, members of society. In other countries, or at all events in England, when a gentleman goes to take up his abode, for a long or a short period, in a strange locality, it is usual for the residents, if they desire to show him any civility, or make his acquaintance, to call upon him in the first instance. In India the reverse is the case. The stranger must make his round of calls, if he wishes to know the residents; and, what is more, he must leave his cards on the mess, 'for the colonel and officers of her Majesty's —— Regiment.'

You may leave a card on every officer in the regiment, from
the senior colonel down to the junior ensign; and each of
them may, and possibly will, invite you to his private board;
but, if you omit to leave a card on the mess, it would be a
gross breach of decorum in any member of the mess to invite
you to dine at the mess-table, because you have 'not left a
card on the mess.' And not only to the royal regiments does
the rule pertain, but to every regiment in India, and to every
brigade of artillery.

Having left my cards at the mess of the regiment to which
my friend belonged, I was driven to the mess-house of the —
— Dragoons, where another expenditure of cards was
incurred; then to the mess-houses of the two native infantry
regiments, and the mess-house of the native cavalry regiment.
I was then whisked off to the house of General Sir Doodle
Dudley, G.C.B., who commanded the division. The General
was very old, close upon eighty; but he was 'made up' to
represent a gentleman of about forty. His chestnut wig fitted
him to perfection, and his whiskers were dyed so adroitly,
that they were an exact imitation of their original colour.
The white teeth were all false; likewise the pink colour in the
cheeks and the ivory hue of the forehead. As for the General's
dress, it fitted him like a glove, and his patent leather boots
and his gold spurs were the neatest and prettiest I had ever
seen. In early life Sir Doodle had been a rival and an
acquaintance of Beau Brummell. When a Colonel in the
Peninsular war, he had been what is called a very good
regimental officer; but, from 1818 until his appointment to
India, in 1847, as a General of Division, he had been

unattached, and had never done a single day's duty. He was so hopelessly deaf, that he never even attempted to ask what was said to him; but a stranger, as I was, would scarcely have credited it; for the General talked, laughed, and rattled on as though he were perfectly unconscious of his infirmity. I ventured a casual remark touching the late dust-storm which had swept over the district, to which the General very vivaciously replied:—

'Yes, my good sir. I knew her in the zenith of her beauty and influence, when she was a lady patroness of Almack's, and the chief favourite of his Royal Highness the Prince Regent. Oh, yes! she is dead, I see by the last overland paper; but I did not think she was so old as they say she was— eighty-four. Only fancy, eighty-four!' Then darting off at a tangent, he remarked, 'I see they give it out that I am to have the command-in-chief at Bombay. The fact is, I don't want Bombay, and so I have told my friends at the Horse Guards at least a dozen times. I want the governorship and the command-in-chief at the Cape; but, if they thrust Bombay upon me, I suppose I must take it. One can't always pick and choose, and I fancy it is only right to oblige now and then.'

'We shall be very sorry to lose you, General,' said my friend, mechanically; 'very sorry indeed.'

'So I have told his Excellency,' exclaimed the General, who presumed that my friend was now talking on an entirely different subject. 'So I have told him. But he will not listen to me. He says that if the court-martial still adheres to its finding of murder, he will upset the whole of the proceedings, and order the man to return to his duty; and the court *will* adhere to its original finding; for the court says, and I say, that a private who deliberately loads his firelock, and deliberately fires at and wounds a serjeant, cannot properly be convicted of manslaughter only. Well, it cannot be helped, I suppose. The fact is, the commander-in-chief is now too old for his work; and he is, as he always was, very obstinate and self-willed.' And the General continued, 'For the command of an army or a division in India, we want men who are not above listening to the advice of the experienced officers by whom they are surrounded!'

When we were leaving the General, he mistook me for my friend and my friend for me, and respectively addressed us accordingly (his eyesight was very imperfect, and he was too vain to wear glasses). He thanked me for having brought my friend to call upon him, and assured my friend that it would afford him the greatest pleasure in the world if the acquaintance, that day made, should ripen into friendship.

'He is an imbecile,' I remarked, when we were driving away from the General's door.

'Yes, and he has been for the last six or seven years,' was the reply.

'But he must be labouring under some delusion with respect to being appointed to the command-in-chief of an Indian presidency?'

'Nothing of the kind. He is certain of it. He will go to Bombay before six weeks are over, you will see.'

The General *did* go to Bombay, where he played such fantastic tricks before high heaven, that the angels could not have 'wept' for laughing at them. Amongst other things, he insisted on the officers of the regiments buttoning their coats and jackets up to the throat, during the hottest time of the year. He would have nothing unmilitary, he said, 'hot climate or no hot climate.' He was quite childish before he relinquished his command, and was brought home just in time to die in his fatherland, and at the country-seat of his aristocratic ancestors. Although utterly unfitted, in his after life, to command troops, he was a very polished old gentleman, externally; and, having enjoyed a very intimate acquaintance with Blücher, and other celebrated commanders, he could repeat many anecdotes of them worthy of remembrance. 'Blücher,' he used to say, 'generally turned into bed all standing, jack-boots included; and, if his valet forgot to take off his spurs, and they became entangled with the sheets, woe betide the valet. The torrent of abuse that he poured forth was something terrific.' I also heard the General say that Blücher, having seen everything in London, remarked with great earnestness, 'Give me Ludgate Hill!' and on being asked to explain why, replied, with reference to the number of jewellers' and silversmiths' shops which in that day decorated the locality,

'Mein Gott! what pillage!'

After leaving the General's house, we called upon some six or eight other magnates of Umballah for the time being; and on returning to the mess-house at the hour of tiffin, I was rather fatigued. The scene, however, revived me considerably. There were seated round the large table, in the centre of the lonely room, some seventy or eighty officers of all ranks, from the various regiments in the station. There was to be a meeting held that day at the mess-room, to discuss some local matter, and the majority of those present had been invited to 'tiff' previously. No one was in uniform— at least, not in military uniform; all wore light shooting-coats and wide-awake hats, covered with turbans. The local question, touching the best means of watering the mall, where the residents used to take their evening ride or drive, having been discussed, the party broke up. Some went to the different billiard-rooms to play matches (for money, of course); others retired to private bungalows to play cards, or read, while reclining on a couch or a bed, or a mat upon the floor. Every one smoked and sipped some sort of liquid. It was to a room in my friend's bungalow that eleven of the party, inclusive of myself, repaired, to while away the time until sundown, by playing whist.

Never did the character of an officer's life in India strike me so forcibly as on that afternoon. There was an air of lassitude and satiety about every one present. The day was hot and muggy, and the atmosphere very oppressive. It was a fatiguing bore to deal the cards, take up the tricks, mark the game, or raise to one's lips the claret cup which Sham had been called upon to brew. Sham was well known to most of the officers of the regiment to which my friend belonged. He had made their acquaintance (to use his own words) when he was on the Governor-General's staff.

The three men who had not cut in at whist were lounging about, and making ineffectual attempts to keep up a conversation. The shooting-coats and the waistcoats were now discarded, and the suspenders, and the shoes, or boots;

in short, each person only wore strictly necessary clothing, while the native (coolie) in the verandah was ever and anon loudly called upon to pull the punkah as strongly as possible. That room that afternoon presented a perfect picture of cantonment life in India during the summer season, between the hours of two and half-past five, p.m. The body is too much exhausted to admit of any serious mental exertion beyond that which sheer amusement can afford; and it is by no means uncommon to find your partner or yourself dropping off to sleep when called upon to lead a card, or follow suit. The three men who were sitting (or lying) out, soon yielded to the influence of the punkah, closed their eyes, and got up a snore, each holding between his fingers the cheroot he had been smoking.

Ah, yes! It is very bad to have to endure the frightful heat—to feel one's blood on the broil, even under a punkah, and with doors and windows closed, to exclude the hot air of the open day. But what must it be for the men, the privates and their wives and children? They have no punkahs, though it has been shown that they might have them at a trifling cost. They have no cold water, much less iced water to sip— though they might have it, if the authorities had the good sense (to put humanity entirely out of the question) to be economical of that invaluable commodity in India, British flesh and blood. They, the men of the ranks, and their wives and children, have no spacious apartments (with well-fitted doors and windows), to move about in, though there is no reason why they should not have them, for the land costs nothing, and labour and material is literally dirt-cheap in the Upper Provinces of India.

'But the Royal Infantry Barracks at Umballah is a fine, large building!' it may be suggested. I reply, 'Not for a regiment one thousand strong'—a regiment mustering one thousand bayonets, to say nothing of the numerous women, and the more numerous children. In a cold climate, it would be ample for their accommodation; but not here, where in a room occupied by an officer, the thermometer frequently stands at ninety-three degrees, and sometimes at one hundred and five degrees. In the matter of ice, the reader must be informed how it is manufactured. During the 'cold weather,' (as the winter is always called,) small earthenware vessels of shallow build, resembling saucers in shape, are filled with water, and placed in an open field, upon a low bed of straw. At dawn of day there is a coating of ice upon each vessel, of about the thickness of a shilling. This is collected by men, women, and children (natives), who receive for each morning's, or hour's work, a sum of money, in cowries, equal to about half of a farthing. When collected, it is carried to an ice-pit, and there stored. The expenses are borne by a subscription, and the amount for each ticket depends entirely on the number of subscribers. In some large stations, an ice-ticket for the hot season costs only three pounds. In smaller stations it will cost six pounds. The amount of ice received by each ticket-holder is about four pounds, and is brought away each morning at daylight, in a canvas bag, enveloped in a thick blanket, by the ticket-holder's own servant. It is then deposited in a basket made expressly for the purpose. In this basket is placed the wine, beer, water, butter, and fruit. The bag of solid ice is in the centre of all these, and imparts to each an equal coldness.

These four pounds of ice, if properly managed, and the air kept out of the basket, will cool an inconceivable quantity of fluids, and will last for twenty-four hours—that is to say, there will be some ice remaining when the fresh bag is brought in. If a bewildered khansamah, or khitmutghur, in his haste to bring a bottle, leaves the basket uncovered, the inevitable consequence is, that the ice melts, and there is an end of it for the day. I have scarcely known a family in which corporal punishment was not inflicted on the servant guilty of such a piece of neglect. But, great as was the privation, it was always cheerfully endured by the society, when the doctors of the various departments indented on them for their shares of ice respectively. And this occasionally happened, when the hospitals were crowded with cases of fever. Scores and scores of lives were often saved by the application of ice to the head, and the administration of cold drinks.

Ice is not manufactured below Benares. Calcutta and its immediate neighbourhood revels in the luxury of American ice, which may be purchased for three half-pence per seer (two pounds). The American ships, trading to India, take it as ballast, which by the time it arrives in the river Hooghley becomes a solid mass.

The sun has gone down, and it is now time to bathe and dress for our evening drive. The band is playing. We descend from the buggy, languidly; and languidly we walk first to one carriage and then to another, to talk with the ladies who are sitting in them. They, the ladies, wear a very languid air, as though life, in such a climate, were a great burden—and it is, no doubt, a great burden from the middle of April to the first

week in October. There is a languid air even about the
liveliest tunes that the band plays. Then we languidly drive to
the mess-house for dinner. The dinner is more a matter of
form than anything else. But the wines, which are well iced,
are partaken of freely enough—especially the champagne.
There is, of course, no intoxication; but as the evening
advances the company becomes more jovial, and by the time
the dessert is placed on the table, that dreadful feeling of
languor has, in a great measure, taken its departure. It is now
that the evening commences, and many very pleasant evenings
have been spent in that Umballah mess-room, despite the
heat. The colonel of the regiment to which my friend belonged
was a man of very good sense; and during the hot season he
sanctioned his officers wearing, except when on parade, a
white twill jacket, of a military cut, with the regimental button;
and he had not the slightest objection to a loose necktie
instead of a tightly-fitting black stock. This matter ought to
have been sanctioned by the highest military authority, the
commander-in-chief; or rather, it ought to have been stated
in a general order that such rational attire was approved of,
instead of being left to the caprice of a colonel, or brigadier,
or general of division. The regiment of royal cavalry, too,
were equally fortunate in their colonel. He was also of opinion
that the comfort of the officers under his command was
worthy of some consideration, and he could not see the
necessity of requiring a gentleman to sit down to dinner in a
thick red cloth jacket (padded), and buttoned up to the very
chin. But before I left Umballah, the old General altered this,
and insisted on 'this loose and unsoldierlike attire being

instantly abandoned.' He had overlooked it for several months, or, at all events, had expressed no objection; but suddenly the Major-General commanding was aroused to observe with great regret that the dress in some regiments was fast becoming subversive, &c., &c. The reason of the Major-General's sudden acuteness of observation was this:— he was about to give a ball at his own house, and for some inexplicable cause had not invited any of the officers of her Majesty's —— Regiment of Foot. But on the morning of the night on which the ball was to take place, he requested his aide-de-camp to write the following note:—

'The Major-General commanding the Division desires that the band of H.M.'s —— Foot may be in attendance at the Major-General's house at half-past nine precisely.'

And the band went at half-past nine, for the General had a perfect right to order the men to attend at his house whenever he pleased; but the band went without their musical instruments, for they (as I believe is the case in all regiments) were the private property of the officers for the time being, and, like the regimental plate, the loan thereof for any particular occasion must be regarded as a matter of favour, and not as a matter of right. So the General had no music out of the band: and the officers in the station had no comfort in their dress, until the General left the station for his command at Bombay.

It may possibly be imagined that the General had, in his earlier days, done the State great service as a military commander, and for that his appointment was the reward. Nothing of the kind. When he left the army, and became unattached, he was only a regimental colonel, and had only been once mentioned by the Duke of Wellington in his despatches, as having gallantly led his regiment into action; for this single mention he was made a brevet Major-General and a C.B., while other colonels who had performed precisely the same service, remained unpromoted and undecorated. Sometimes, during his Indian career—not that he was intoxicated by wine, for the General in his dotage was rather abstemious—he would be utterly oblivious to the fact that he *was* in India, and would hold a conversation with some young ensign, (who had been one of his dinner party, and who, in haste to get away early to billiards, came up to say good night) after the following fashion:—

'Look here, my pretty boy, as you will be passing Fribourg and Pontet's, just look in and tell them—O, how like you are to your dear mother! I can remember her when she was thought, and truly, to be one of the prettiest women in all Europe! Charming eyes—lovely complexion! Well, look in at Fribourg and Pontet's.'

'Yes, General.'

'And tell them to send me a canister of the Duke of Kent's mixture. O! how very like you are to your dear mother, my pretty boy! The last they sent me had scent in it. Tell them I hate scent in snuff.'

'Yes, General.'

'O! how VERY like you are to your dear mother!'

(The General had never seen the boy's mother in the course of his long and useless life.)

'Yes, General.'

'Well, do not forget the snuff.'

'O, no, General! Good night.'

'God bless thee, my pretty boy! O! how like you are to your dear mother!'

I do not mean to say that General Sir Doodle Dudley was an average specimen of the General officers sent out by the Horse Guards to command divisions in India. That would be untrue: for some, though very old and inefficient, could see, hear, and understand. But within the past ten years, some others that I know of have been sent out, to Bengal alone, who were not one whit more efficient than General Sir Doodle Dudley.

The nights being more enjoyable, comparatively, than the days, no wonder that they are rarely given up for sleep by the majority of military men or younger civilians in India. Of course, married men with families must, and do, for the most part, lead regular lives, or, at all events, conform to some fixed domestic rules. But it is not so with the unmarried, who take their rest (sleep) much in the same way that inveterate drunkards take their drink—'little and often.' You will see a young officer playing at billiards at half-past two or three in the morning, and at five you will see him on the parade-ground with his company. He has had his sleep and his bath, and, to use his own words, he 'feels as fresh as a three-year-old.' Between seven and twelve he will also have an hour or so of 'the balmy,' and then, after tiffin, he will perhaps get a few winks while reading the newspaper or a book, or while sitting on the bench in the billiard-room, 'watching the game.' Have these young men, it may be asked, nothing to do? Have they no occupation? Yes. They have to keep themselves alive and in good spirits, and that is no easy task either, in the hot weather of the Upper Provinces. Some of them (a few) in the East India Company's Service will take to studying the languages, in the hope that proficiency therein will lead to staff employ. Those, however, who do not happen to have good interest to back their claims soon find out that the order of the Governor-General in Council touching a knowledge of the Native languages is a mere sham; and that ignorance clothed with interest is—so far as advancement in life is concerned—far preferable to a well-stored head and a steady character.